COURTING JULIET

BROTHERHOOD PROTECTORS WORLD

PAM MANTOVANI

Twisted Page Press LLC

BROTHERHOOD PROTECTORS

ORIGINAL SERIES BY ELLE JAMES

Brotherhood Protectors Series
Montana SEAL (#1)
Bride Protector SEAL (#2)
Montana D-Force (#3)
Cowboy D-Force (#4)
Montana Ranger (#5)
Montana Dog Soldier (#6)
Montana SEAL Daddy (#7)
Montana Ranger's Wedding Vow (#8)
Montana SEAL Undercover Daddy (#9)
Cape Cod SEAL Rescue (#10)
Montana SEAL Friendly Fire (#11)
Montana SEAL's Bride (#12)
Montana Rescue
Hot SEAL, Salty Dog

For Aunti Mar, who introduced me to my hero and gave me my own HappilyEverAfter

ACKNOWLEDGMENTS

My profound thanks go to Elle James. Your unrelenting support and encouragement is valuable beyond words.

To the readers who take time out of their busy lives to read my books. Thank you. I hope my words bring you joy and pleasure.

To my brother-in-law Jon, who has always insisted that I'd sell more books if I just killed someone. It seemed only fair that I named the villain after him.

To my family who continue to believe in me. I love you all more than there are words.

As always, to Denny, my life would be empty and incomplete without you. I'm so grateful you made that third phone call.

CHAPTER 1

With a mug of hot tea cradled in her hands, Juliet Ethridge watched dawn lighten the big sky Montana was famous for. Her body clock was still on New York time.

She didn't regret the move here – only the reason for it. What she did hate was admitting she'd run from a man. She'd tried for months to ignore the stalking, had followed all the advice to alter her schedule to make it harder for him to keep track of her. When she'd found herself ignoring invitations and staying in her apartment for days on end, she'd known something had to change.

In spite of the fear he'd brought into her life, she would miss the impromptu dinners and shopping excursions with her mother, the occasional date, attending the theatre where she'd all but grown up. With a small smile, she admitted she would also miss the luxury of take out and dining in her favorite restaurants. She also believed this move would prove good for her, giving her time to reflect on where she was in her life.

With that in mind she took in her surroundings. As if on cue, an elk stepped out of the woods that ringed the undulating grassy perimeter.

"Oh," she whispered. "Look at you. Don't move."

Keeping her gaze on the grazing elk – and she'd have to rethink her initial plan of putting a garden in that spot – she set down her mug and reached for her cell phone.

"I promise this is the only way I'll shoot you."

With a few swipes, she zoomed in and clicked off a succession of photos. Delighted, she sent them in a text message to her mother. In less than thirty seconds, her phone chimed, the sound chasing the elk back into the woods.

"Momma," Juliet laughed. "Your call chased him away. But wasn't he just beautiful?"

"And here I was worried about how you were handling your first morning in the wild."

Juliet laughed again, sipped her tea. "Montana is hardly the wild."

"It's not New York," her mother said. "And it lured my baby girl far away from me."

Of course her mother, a Broadway legend, wanted to protect her. But Margot Ramsey Ethridge's fame couldn't keep the stalker from continuing to hound Juliet. "We both know that's not true."

"You're right, that crazy author is what sent you there."

As much as it pained Juliet to admit author Jon Hock's obsession with her was responsible for her new living status, she didn't want her mother to worry. "You know I wanted a change of scenery. Somewhere I could set up my own recording studio, somewhere I can focus and work on the current books I'm contracted to narrate. A quiet place to prep my voice and hone my technique if I hope to get cast in the upcoming animated movie."

"Of course they'll want you."

"I love you, Momma."

"Maybe you'll meet a handsome cowboy while you're there."

"Think again." Juliet's protest echoed with laughter. "I'm here to work, not have a romance."

"I was working, not looking for a romance when I met your father."

Juliet pictured her father in one of his tailored business suits, so quiet and steady in contrast to her mother's outgoing personality. "I tell you what, if I run across a cowboy who can show me the kind of love you and Daddy share I'll snatch him right up."

"There's nothing I'd wish more for you my darling."

Hanging up a short time later, Juliet drained her cup of now-cold tea. And had her second surprise arrival of the morning.

Her heart thudded hard in trepidation, her breath backed up in her lungs, and her legs quivered so hard that she knew she couldn't stand. Or run. Her hand reached for her phone, only she didn't lift it. She held on, her thumb poised over the emergency button. She hated knowing she did so out of a sense of unease. There'd been a time when she would have welcomed without hesitation the chance to meet someone new, a time when her first thought didn't center on fear or thoughts of her safety.

Then, as the arrival came closer, as she got her first good look at him, everything within her calmed. Except her heart, which continued to pound. For very different reasons. . .

He rode the horse as comfortably as she'd ridden in cabs. He wore jeans with a plaid shirt, black boots to match the cowboy hat shading his face.

"Morning," he called out, reining the horse to a stop about three feet from where Juliet sat on the porch. "Are you Juliet Ethridge?"

"Who's asking?"

He grinned while his hand took one long soothing stroke down the horse's neck. Juliet's cheeks heated as she had thoughts that were as inappropriate as they were unexpected for a total stranger. And yet, she couldn't dismiss them. "Sounds like a city girl, alright."

"And you still haven't answered my question."

He removed his hat, charming her with the old fashioned manners. Although cut shorter than she might have expected of a cowboy, his hair was a mixture of blonde and brown to go with eyes as warm and brown as melted chocolate.

"I'm Walker Grant. Sadie McClain, that is Sadie Paterson, asked me to look in on your livestock for you."

Juliet relaxed a little. She'd worked with Sadie before and the actress had been the one who'd called her with the news of this property being available for purchase. Then, she blinked. "I have livestock?"

With his hat he gestured to her left. A short distance away stood a structure even a city girl recognized as a barn.

"You've got two young stallions to go along with a milk cow and some chickens."

"Horses, a cow and chickens," she murmured before she laughed. "Imagine that."

"Uh, Sadie mentioned I should suggest you keep me on to manage the ranch and stock. I know Avery Sawyer is hoping you'll let her mate her mares with your stallions. I have some experience helping out in that area." He glanced around, looked back at her. "Carl and Esther kind of let everything run down a bit before they sold the place to you. I can help get it patched up and shining. You've got the potential for a nice place here." Again he used his hat to direct her attention. "There's a small cabin not very far from here."

"You'd live here?"

"If it's alright with you." He shifted in the saddle, kept his gaze steady on hers. Juliet realized she'd been leaning toward him a little. "You can ask Sadie and Avery about me."

She wasn't sure how she felt about this man, any man, living in her backyard so to speak. And yet she didn't experience any of the trepidation or mistrust that had been her constant companions before leaving New York. She took another survey of him, at the corded neck and broad shoulders that hinted at muscle. More strong muscles flexed in his thighs as he kept the horse still. Long fingers kept a loose grip on the reins. Juliet shivered a little at the memory of watching one hand take that slow stroke of the horse.

It wasn't just his looks, although yes, there would be the bonus of having someone attractive to look at every day. It defied all reasoning, and certainly she couldn't explain it, but she felt a kind of connection with Walker Grant. For the first time in months she was reminded she was the kind of woman who enjoyed men, who liked to flirt and have these fluttery feelings in her stomach. And stronger needs pulsing lower in her body.

That didn't mean anything would come of these feelings. Simply because Walker Grant would be working and living close by didn't mean he was attracted to her. But, God, it felt wonderful to feel normal again.

"I'd like to change and have you show me around a little." She stood, grinning when her stomach rumbled. "I also need something to eat. Come in and we'll talk while I cook breakfast."

She started to turn away, only to pause and watch as he dismounted. He moved with a fluid grace that didn't diminish the power of his body. After tethering the horse, he came up two steps, putting them on eye level. And oh, she had her answer about his feelings and then some.

The warmth of his brown eyes beckoned her to step forward, to do more than flirt or talk ranch business. The look he gave her promised heat along with caring, gentleness that could give way to rushed passion.

She stood, motionless, waiting to see what would happen.

WALKER HELD his body rigid as he met Juliet's gaze. Otherwise he thought he'd scoop her into his arms and carry her to the first available flat surface. Horizontal or vertical, her body under or over his, it made no difference to him. As long as his hands were free to roam her curves and his mouth had access to all kinds of interesting places until he buried deep inside her.

If he'd read the interest in her eyes right – and he was damn sure he had – she'd go along with the idea.

He'd been given a photo of her before he came here today so he knew she had light brown shoulder length hair that looked like silk. He knew her eyes were also brown and that her lips naturally curved up at each end. She had a sprinkle of freckles across her nose and upper cheeks.

He should have been better prepared for the sight of her. She looked like a fresh-faced girl-next-door. Only, the reality had far surpassed photos and was worlds away from wholesomeness. His body had tightened and not relaxed one iota since he arrived. It didn't help any that he could tell she wore no bra under the long-sleeve thermal shirt.

"Can I offer you a cup of tea?" She gestured with the empty mug in her hand. "Since I didn't know to expect you, I didn't stock any coffee. Tea's better for my throat and voice."

He cocked his head, feigning ignorance. "Are you a singer?"

"No." She laughed a little. "That's my mother's expertise, along with acting on stage. I do voice-overs, narration. Audio books." A shadow clouded her eyes at the mention of audio books. The reason she'd escaped New York. He knew the source of that shadow. And had been hired to guard her should the source find its way here.

"So, you get paid to read books."

"It's a little more involved than that, but I guess that's a basic description."

He climbed a step. Juliet took a small move in

retreat. He climbed again. This time she held ground. "Is this your vacation house?"

"No," she said. God, he could imagine that little breathless catch to her voice as he thrust inside her. "I had a studio built on the back of the house. I'll be doing all my recording here."

"I'm always interested in electronics," he said, leaning back against the railing that edged the steps up to the porch. "And while I'd like a tour of your studio, right now, I should get over to the barn and see to the animals."

Unfortunately there hadn't been enough time between his hiring and her arrival to set up cameras or listening devices. So, he was thankful when she nodded agreement without any questions. He needed to get the lay of the land, so to speak, but also a look at what he could do to keep an eye and ear on her at all times.

Until he could find a way to get inside her house and plant some devices there, he'd settle for examining the barn. Lifting his hat in a salute, he placed it on his head and headed down the steps.

"I'll be in the barn if you need anything."

AN HOUR LATER, Juliet ventured outside. A call to

Sadie had confirmed Walker Grant was who he claimed. She'd also vouched for his honor. Since Sadie had her own experience dealing with a stalker, Juliet had agreed with her point that having Walker around the ranch would put her mind at ease.

With the roof of the back porch shielding her from the sun, Juliet paused. The sky was incredibly bright and blue with only a few cotton tuffs of clouds. It was so quiet, nothing at all like the constant drum of traffic and noise she was used to in New York.

She'd come to Montana to escape a monster. And while Walker Grant had been a surprise, a very attractive one, she'd also come here to work and live. Living here meant getting to know people. Trusting them. Time to start. She'd allowed one man to force her into running. She wouldn't allow another.

Stepping off the back porch, she crossed the yard. At the open barn door she paused. The interior might be brighter than she expected, but even her city nose picked up the scents of hay and manure. It hit her then just how truly she'd left the city behind. And hopefully the man who'd terrorized her the past year.

As she studied the interior, she saw there were three stalls on the right side and two on the left. At the end of the wide aisle, on the left at the rear of the barn, there appeared to be a room of some sort. She could hear murmuring, a low comforting tone that brought to mind whispered conversations in bed.

Something brushed her leg just as she took a step forward. Jumping a little at the unexpected sensation, she looked down, her hammering heart going still. "Well, hello." She crouched and ran a hand over the back of the ginger-colored cat. A few strokes later she discovered a heavy belly.

"That's Molly."

Juliet looked up to see Walker approach. She took note that he kept space between them. The way he also kept his hands in the front pockets of his jeans meant she had an unobstructed view of his cock. She shivered a little, speculating how it would feel to be pressed against him. Walker took a miniscule step in retreat.

"She'll be giving you some more barn cats in a few weeks."

"Barn cats?"

"They live out here, keeping mice away." He smiled a little. "The horses seem to like having them around."

"Pet pals." She chuckled at her bad joke. With one last stroke of the cat, she stood.

He may have taken a small step away but they were still standing close. Closer than she'd wanted to be with any man other than her father for far longer than she could recall. Walker kept his gaze steady on hers, his brown eyes filled with interest. His lips were firm and she couldn't help but wonder how they would feel on hers. And anywhere else he might like to linger.

And oh wasn't it glorious to see interest in a man's eyes rather than obsession in a crazed man's gaze?

"Do you have time to give me a tour of my barn?"

"You're the boss."

"Oh, I don't think so. At least not in this arena." She pointed a finger at her chest, felt the heat of a thrill zip through her when his gaze lowered to take in the gesture. "City girl, remember?" His gaze rose and she once again found herself pinned by the intensity of his eyes.

He didn't look much like a ranch hand at the moment. With broad shoulders and strong chest muscles a flannel shirt couldn't disguise he looked like the kind of man you could depend on, the kind of man who would honor his promises and defend you against an enemy.

The romantic part of her heart that never lost hope of finding a lifelong partner sighed with pleasure.

She turned and headed to the first stall where a majestic black horse stood.

"This is Scotty," Walker said as he came to a stop beside her.

Juliet took in the elegant, regal way the horse held his head. "That sounds much too pedestrian a name for such a beauty." She grinned when the horse lowered his head a little in agreement. "Looks like he agrees with me."

"Oh, our Scotty thinks highly of himself."

"How could he not? I might be from the city but even I recognize a magnificent animal when I see one." In the silence that followed, she realized how her comment could be taken. She felt heat flood her cheeks. "What I mean is . . . "

"I know what you mean." Chuckling, he lifted his free hand to scratch at the horse's forehead. At least she thought that was what it was called. Walker shifted to look at her, his brown eyes warm and clear, an enticing invitation to move closer and feel that hand stroke down her back.

When she realized she'd been about to lean into him, she cleared her throat. "You mentioned someone wants to breed their horse with mine?"

"Yes, Avery Sawyer. She and her husband are your neighbors."

"I'm going to guess they're a little further away than the apartment across the hall that I'm used to."

He smiled and gestured her toward another stall. "Avery's ranch is little more than five miles to the west."

"Five miles. And this morning I sent Momma a photo of an elk in my front yard." She shook her head. "My life has taken a drastic turn. Now, who is this?" This horse was a light caramel color in contrast to the darkness of the first, but no less imposing.

"This is Captain."

"Captain," she repeated. She glanced around. "These are the only two?"

"So far." He nodded toward the empty stalls. "You have room to add more. Plenty of pasture for grazing. You could build yourself a tidy little stud service here."

She choked at the suggestion. From the corner of her eye, because God she could not look at him, she saw his lips curve in a grin. Crossing the wide aisle she trailed a fingertip along the leather strap of some sort hanging from another stall. Another reminder of how her life had changed. She hoped, prayed, she'd left more than family and city life behind. She wanted to be able to enjoy living here, trying new experiences. Not being afraid of having an unbalanced man threatening her.

"So, instead of being a horse whisperer, I'll be a horse madam."

He chuckled as he approached to stand beside her. "That's one hell of a way to look at it. But, yeah, I guess you could say that." He shifted so he leaned his left arm on top of the stall's half door and faced her.

"I can handle the stud services for you."

CHAPTER 2

SHE REFUSED TO REACT, refused to consider he meant anything more than breeding the horses.

It didn't stop her from wondering, imagining, wanting. Still, determined to maintain a poised impression, she lifted her chin.

"Well, I moved out here because I wanted a change in my life. Looks like I've got it." She held out her hand. "I guess you're hired."

His hand closed around hers, held on for just a breath longer than needed. "I won't let you down." She wasn't sure why, and maybe it had more to do with the sharp look in his eyes rather than tone of voice, but it sounded like more than a promise to work hard.

"So, what happens now?" she asked, sliding her

hand free of his. She shivered at the way skin rubbed against skin.

"I'll finish up here, call Avery and discuss the breeding with her." He shrugged. "I guess you go back to your studio."

"I didn't really plan on working today." She glanced around. "There must be something I can do around here." She looked back at him. "If I'm going to own a ranch, I should know something about it."

He tipped his head at her. "Those clothes aren't really suited for ranch work."

"I have others."

"I bet you do."

She narrowed her gaze. "Is that a crack about women and clothes?"

"It's a statement based on my experience."

"Had much experience with women have you?" She walked toward the barn door. He followed.

"A gentleman never tells."

They walked out into the sunshine just as a delivery truck approached. Juliet shivered when Walker inched closer to her. "Were you expecting anything?" he asked.

"Juliet Ethridge?" the driver asked after he slid the door open. She nodded. "Delivery for you. From New York."

"Momma," she whispered and felt Walker relax next to her. "Momma must have sent me something."

The driver drew a cellophane wrapped wire basket out of the truck. Inside were bricks of cheese, grapes, boxes of crackers, a bottle of champagne and two glasses nestled on pink confetti paper. He handed the basket to Juliet, who then passed it to Walker so she could sign for the delivery. "If you'll wait a minute, I'll go inside and get your tip."

He blinked in surprise. "That's not necessary." With a nod, he returned to the truck and, with a quick honk of the horn, turned around and drove off.

"Another difference between here and New York," Juliet commented before turning to Walker and reaching for the tiny envelope attached to the end of the ribbon. "Momma knows this is my favorite deli." She slipped the card free of the envelope, then froze. Her knees trembled, her fingers curled the edge of the card, a moan scraped past her pressed lips. Walker lowered the basket to the ground.

"Juliet?" She stepped back when she saw his hands lift, as if to reach for her. "It isn't from your mother." The statement, not a question, had her lifting her face, looking at him. In complete defiance of all she'd been through, all she still feared, she said nothing, and offered the card. She didn't need him to read the card aloud to recall the words.

For our reunion celebration. See you soon.

"How could he know where I am?" Temper crept in to replace the numbness. "How did he find me?"

"This came from a deli, like you said. Let's call them." He gestured to the house. "You can tell me what's going on."

She resisted the temptation to race inside, it felt too much like running. She also decided to trust Walker with the truth. After all, she'd just hired him to work here. It made sense that she be honest. He needed to be aware of the situation.

"As I told you, I do book narrations, voice-overs, that sort of thing. Have you heard of Jon Hock?"

"The author?" he asked and she nodded, rubbed a hand over her tumbling stomach. "He writes crime fiction." Walker followed her as she walked to the house. "Some of it's pretty graphic."

"It didn't start that way. The first couple of books were standard crime fiction. After I was contracted for the first novel, he requested me for the next three."

"He became fixated on you."

"I just thought he liked my reading style. Then." She trailed off as they reached the back door, as Walker held it open for her. Once inside, she moved to the stove, turned on the burner beneath the tea kettle. When she reached for the tea bag, and realized her hand shook, she closed it into a fist and drew in several deep breaths. "The novels became more violent. Much more graphic, especially in scenes that involved sexual violence toward women. I just couldn't stomach what I was reading."

"You refused to narrate his latest book."

"I cancelled our contract, returned the fee. I thought that would be the end of it." She put a tea bag in a mug, looked up at Walker, who shook his head in answer to her silent question. "Water? There's also some orange juice in the fridge."

"Water would be great."

Rather than hand over the bottled water, she opened a cabinet, drew down a clear goblet. Scooping ice out of the freezer, she poured the water and turned to hand the glass to him. She caught, but ignored, the smirk.

"He didn't take your cancellation well," Walker said after draining half the glass.

"It started with a letter to my agent, pleading that I reconsider. There was a promise of additional money. Next was a delivery of Calla Lilies. Somehow he'd learned they're my favorite. Before long I started receiving phone calls, telling me I was his muse and he hadn't been able to write since learning I didn't want to read his words. Sometimes he only cried."

She jumped a little when the tea kettle began whistling. Pouring the hot water, dipping the bag, stirring in honey, all combined to settle her a little. Wrapping both hands around the mug, she leaned against the counter and studied Walker as she sipped her tea.

Something about him calmed her. As strange as it might be, especially coming from a born and bred New Yorker, she trusted this stranger. God knew he looked strong enough, capable enough to handle whatever came his way. But there was something about the softness of his brown eyes that assured her she was safe whenever he was around.

"I assume you contacted the police."

She winced. "Not at first. I thought if I ignored him he'd move on. Instead, gifts and letters came more frequently. He routinely followed me. At first he would simply stay a small distance away and watch."

"At first."

"Yes."

"What changed?"

"He became more aggressive and his pleas took on a darker tone. He made threats."

She recalled all the days, weeks, months of

anxious nerves, the attempts to ignore the threats, the search of mind and soul when a move became unavoidable. The ache of saying goodbye to her parents. Suddenly it all crashed down on her, made her acutely aware of everything she'd lost or given up. To her horror, tears blurred her vision.

"I tried staying inside, not going out where he'd be able to approach me. Only one night as she came out of the theatre, he confronted my mother."

"So you came here."

"I came here thinking if I got away he'd forget me." Her chest rose and fell as her breathing accelerated with dread.

"You came here," he repeated, walking toward her. "To protect your mother." Gently he took her into his arms.

"I ran here."

"You came here to make a new life." His lips brushed hers.

She nearly groaned at the warmth and softness of his mouth on hers. It felt right, so very right, and she wanted this kiss to go on and on. She'd settled, she realized, the instant he'd wrapped her in his embrace. However, he paused, his lips hovering over hers. "It's never going to end. I'm never going to be rid of him," she whispered, suddenly more afraid of losing the taste of him.

"You don't have to worry." He kissed her gently. "I'm here." His kiss was a little longer this time. "I'll protect you."

WALKER COULD HAVE ARGUED that he'd kissed Juliet to settle her down, to soothe the nerves that were building. It would be a lie. He kissed her because he wanted to, had wanted to since his first sight of her. He wanted to know the feel of her mouth under his, wanted to know her taste, the feel of her body pressed to him as tightly as their lips now clung.

Perfect.

Her mouth fit to his as if his second half, her taste held the hint of tea and honey, and the feel of her body against his had him aching to take her to bed. She thought herself weak for having moved here. He thought her courageous. Even now, when distress had enabled him to get past her barriers, she held her own. She didn't passively accept his kiss, didn't stand by limp. She kissed him back, made the first move that resulted in their tongues tangling. Her hands slid around his waist, her arms tightening, holding him close. The strength of her response told him more than either of them had expected.

For a variety of reasons, kissing her wasn't smart.

He didn't hold her just in comfort against the fear she so openly expressed. God knows his body didn't feel all that comfortable with her pressed against him.

Because he did like it, because he wanted even more, he slowly ended the kiss and lifted his mouth from hers. Her wet swollen lips tested his resolve. Her eyes, when the lashes lifted, were clouded with desire that slowly shifted to shock.

"I'm not going to apologize," he said. Though he probably should, but he'd been drawn to her and damn but she'd responded so hotly sweet.

With a slight lift of her chin, a talent he admired and wondered if she'd inherited from her mother, she found her balance. "Neither will I."

"Good, then you won't mind when I kiss you again."

"*If* you kiss me again, it will be because I invite you to do so."

"Whenever you want."

She eased out of his hold. "I didn't come here for a romance. I came to start a new life."

"No reason you can't do both."

Her lips trembled with a grin. "You're a cocky son of a gun, aren't you?"

"Honest," he corrected, staring deep into her eyes. "I'm attracted to you, Juliet. And if that kiss was any indication, you're attracted to me." He reached for her hand, held on when she made a half-hearted attempt to pull free. "I meant what I said. I'll do whatever it takes to protect you. I'm also going to do my best to kiss you again. Soon."

When she narrowed her gaze, he released her hand, stepped back. "For now, let's call this deli and see what we can find out."

It took multiple phone calls, aided by suggestions from Walker as to what questions Juliet should ask. Finally, they found their answer.

"You're not surprised," she said, her fingers tapping on the pad of paper where she'd meticulously taken notes on every step of every conversation.

"A couple of possibilities crossed my mind. Just bad damn luck that the girl at the shipping company is an aspiring author and fan of his writing."

"She gave him my information, in direct defiance of my request for privacy."

The clerk had given her stalker the address where Juliet had shipped some of her personal belongings. Still, he didn't like hearing the writer had been close enough to Juliet's apartment to learn which moving company she'd used.

"In return, he gave her an autographed book,

along with the promise to read and critique her novel," Walker said.

"She sold my privacy and peace of mind for a few words on a page."

"If it's any comfort at least you know she'll have plenty of time to read that book of his since her lapse in judgement got her fired."

"I'll make sure I think of that when Jon Hock shows up on my doorstep."

The words sent a chill down his spine, reminding him of how her life had been the last year before she'd moved here. He covered her hand with his. "He won't get that close."

"You can't know that." She jerked her hand free, stood, paced. "You can't promise that."

"I can." He rose, faced her.

"What are you going to do? Move in here, be by my side twenty-four-seven?"

"What a terrific idea. Which room is yours?"

He nearly grinned at the way color flared onto her cheeks. "You are not staying in my room." She drew in an unsteady breath. "You're not staying by my side. I have work. You have livestock to tend. I won't be watched over like a two-year old."

But she would be. He'd been hired to insure her safety. The trick would be to do so without her suspecting he was doing more than working on her ranch.

SIX HOURS LATER, Juliet shut down the recording machinery. All in all she didn't know why she'd bothered. She knew herself well enough to have expected the morning's activities would impact her narration. At times her voice had quivered. Other times her pacing had been off.

"Damn Jon Hock." And while she was at it, "Damn Walker Grant."

It galled her pride to admit thoughts of Walker, their kiss and his claim of moving into her bedroom had hovered in her mind the rest of the day. What shocked her was the idea of letting him do just that.

She didn't behave this way. She'd never been so impulsive where a man was involved. If she followed through on this unexpected attraction she'd be going to bed with a stranger, trusting him with an intimacy she rarely shared with anyone.

Was it simply lust, a physical craving that sprang from the emotional upheaval of having moved halfway across the country? Who knew? Who cared?

She rose, stretched her back, rolled her shoulders

as she walked over to stare out the window that overlooked the barn area.

Hadn't she come here wanting to recapture control over her life? What better way than to accept and use this heated need she felt for him to escape for a small time?

EXCEPT, she couldn't. She wasn't a virgin, but she wanted, had always wanted, romance more than sex. Okay, what she really wanted was both, along with a healthy dose of respect, in one package. This rushed need she had for Walker wasn't like her. She preferred a slower approach to intimacy. Old-fashioned, her friends often teased. When you've grown up watching your parents court and romance one another on a daily basis, what else would you want but the same?

Right now she wanted a glass of wine. Leaving the studio, she crossed into the kitchen and stopped short. Her heart lurched, then raced. Walker stood at the sink, the sleeves of his shirt rolled up to reveal muscled forearms while he washed something under the water stream of the faucet.

"What are you doing?"

He shot her a look over his shoulder. "Done for the day?" Thrown off center, she nodded and he turned back to the sink. "I looked in your refrigerator and didn't see much more than stuff for salad so I rode over to my place." He turned off the water, shook his hands, ripped a paper towel off the dispenser and turned to face her. With shock she realized he wore a gun in a holster at his waist. Her gaze lifted to his. She could ask, she could demand he remove and secure the weapon. She chose to ignore it and the reason why he felt compelled to wear it.

"I thought steaks on the grill and baked potatoes to go with the salad," he said.

"You're making me dinner?"

"Us."

She'd had men try to seduce her over dinner, one they'd taken her to, even a time or two one they'd ordered in. But no one had ever taken the time to do the duty himself. Looking at him a little more closely she realized he wore different clothes than earlier today, and he appeared to have shaved.

She pressed a hand to the flutter in her stomach, refusing to lower her gaze to the gun. "Do I have time to go upstairs and freshen up?"

"We've got all night."

The suggestion, delivered in a low seductive tone, had the flutter in her stomach ramping up to a full-blown tremor.

"I'm hungry," she said before turning to walk away. Her steps faltered when he spoke in the kind of soft whisper lovers used when tangled together.

"So am I."

She deliberately held thoughts at bay while she changed. After far too much indecision, she settled on loose linen slacks and a sleeveless top. For herself, she argued. She needed something to help her relax after a stressful day. She brushed her hair, spritzed on scent but avoided a make-up refresh. She re-entered the kitchen to find a candle on the set table, soft music circling the room, and Walker pouring wine.

"I spoke with Avery today," he said, offering the crystal glass.

Her gaze went from the glass to the bottle on the counter. The bottle that had been in the package delivered earlier today. She also realized there was a platter of cheese and crackers waiting.

"I thought about pouring it down the drain." He paused until she lifted her gaze to his. "Then I decided it would chap his butt if he knew you were sharing all this with me."

"I like that thought." She reached for the glass. His fingers covered hers on the stem, lingered a heartbeat before he released his hold.

"Avery's thrilled you're willing to breed your

horses with hers." He reached for his wine glass. "She also invited us to dinner."

"Us?"

"Us," he confirmed, taking a long swallow. "Unless you want to take a greater interest in learning the ins and outs of horse breeding."

She shuddered. "No, I'm fine with knowing you're handling the details."

She hoped to make new friends and wanted to accept the invitation. Only, it went without saying that Walker would also come. And that was the crux of the problem. Already she was becoming far too accustomed to his presence. With a small shake of her head she decided she'd worry about it later. Tonight she wanted to relax, enjoy a glass, maybe two of this excellent wine, and let a sexy man cook her dinner.

Her brows knitted as she took a deep sip. She wasn't going to relax if she continued to think of Walker as sexy. On the other hand there was no denying her hormones found him very appealing.

"Something wrong?"

She looked up to see he stood close. Her mouth went dry. Those warm chocolate eyes tempted her to rise up and take a big tasty bite of him. "No," she said, dragging her mind back to reality instead of indulging in fantasy.

"To eventful days." She toasted him with her glass. "And quiet ones."

"And evenings," he suggested, flashing an appealing grin before he sipped his wine.

"You're deliberately baiting me."

"Not at all. I'm being honest." His grin vanished and his eyes suddenly looked sharp and penetrating. "I'm telling you that I'm attracted to you."

She knew he wasn't saying this, looking at her like this to take her mind off the package that had been delivered, or the threat it implied. He was, exactly as he said, being honest. Walker Grant looked at her the way a man looked at a woman he wanted to take to bed. And that woman would be thankful every day of her life for the experience.

Her stomach coiled tight. It had been so long since a man had looked at her this way. Longer still since she'd looked back. She couldn't recall ever feeling an attraction, a physical need, so quickly before.

God help her, she wanted to reach for him, take him upstairs and do every wicked thing she could imagine.

His gaze continued to hold hers as he set down his glass, took hers from suddenly nerveless fingers.

"I can be patient," he said, drawing her close. "I have a feeling you'll be worth the wait." His hands circled her, pressed her against him before rising to tangle in her hair. Holding her in place. The fact that he did so with care knocked at her heart. She had little to no resistance to tenderness. "But, God, I really want a taste of you now."

CHAPTER 3

His tone had been rough, but his mouth was gentle as he covered hers. His lips meshed to hers, took from hers, gave to hers. Whether long, drawn-out kisses or tiny nibbles he continued to slowly and softly seduce her. Even when his tongue tempted her to part her lips, to tangle hers with his, he continued this leisurely assault on her senses. She quivered as she thought of other places where he could use that very talented tongue. While he held her, he made no other move to release this need building inside of her. She thought she might explode if he didn't touch her. So it was she who reached for him, drew his hand up to cup her breast.

Both of them moaned at this first touch.

His palm kneaded, his fingers plucked at her rigid nipple. Her knees nearly gave out. Before she could beg him to do more, he ended the kiss, his mouth hovering over hers.

"Juliet." Feeling the warmth of his breath against her mouth, she leaned forward, tasted the fast pulse at his throat. "God, stop. Before I can't. Look at me."

That first hint of urgency had her opening her eyes. His bore into her, not with anger but a pleading.

"Tonight's not right." Even through his grimace she could see the brightness of humor. "Well, it damn sure feels right, but the timing sucks." He lowered his forehead to hers, drew in a deep breath. "I don't think either one of us is ready for what's happening here."

"I didn't come here." She used the tip of her tongue to moisten her lips, wondered how soon she could have another sample of him. "Looking for romance."

She felt the chill before he released her and stepped back. "Sweetheart, romance isn't what I'm talking about." He reached for his wine, took a healthy swallow.

"A one-night stand."

"No." His hand snaked out to hold her in place. The disappointment that soured her stomach faded at his abrupt denial. "I'm definitely going to want more than one night with you." His hand squeezed once, then released her. "It's not personal, Juliet. God knows it's not you. I'm not good for any kind of long run. I don't get attached."

She noted he'd turned away, hadn't looked at her while making the statement. She wanted to appreciate his honesty, his warning that whatever they shared she should know, upfront, it would come to an end. And yet her heart constricted a little.

"Very well. We'll just take each day as it comes." With a casualness her mother had used in her first starring role, Juliet reached for her wine, took a long sip. Made sure she looked at him. "In the meantime, let's have some of that cheese."

While the potatoes baked, they sat outside, nibbling on cheese and watching the spectacular sun set. Juliet marveled that this was a view she'd see often. Walker teased her about not seeing the sun through the mountain of snow winter would bring. Over dinner, she further enjoyed his company, laughed at some of his stories of growing up here in Eagle Rock, and was charmed by insights into people he said she should expect to meet. At one point, she marveled at how comfortable – outside of the intense physical attraction – she felt with him. There were small touches and more than a few long looks. By time he announced it was time for him to leave, Juliet wondered what it would be like to walk upstairs rather than to the door with him.

"Thank you for dinner." Her mouth quirked. "And for watching while I did the dishes."

"Hey, I cooked."

"So you argued."

"I didn't argue." He leaned down and nipped at her lips. "I made my point." Before she could draw breath he gathered her close and kissed her. By time he ended the kiss her ears were ringing. Before she could clear her thoughts enough to find the words to ask him to stay he stepped away.

"Make sure you lock the door behind me." She blinked as he stepped over the threshold, closed the door. "Juliet," he called out. "Lock the door. Turn on your alarm."

"Maybe I don't want to."

She imagined more than heard his sigh. "Tonight's not the right night." A pause. "You know it."

She hesitated, then reached out and threw the bolt. "I hate that you're right."

"So do I."

WALKER SCANNED the horizon as he approached Juliet's ranch. Bad enough he'd hardly slept for remembering the feel of her in his arms, the taste of her as she returned his kisses. Even speaking with her mother after arriving at the bunkhouse, hearing the Broadway legend's distress when he relayed the details about the package delivery, hadn't been enough to stop him from wishing he'd stayed the night with the appealing Juliet.

He'd awoken this morning with vivid dreams lingering in his mind. And a throbbing hard dick that had needed a cold shower and his hand before he could think of getting dressed. Now he swore when he saw the lights were on upstairs. She was still in her bedroom.

Needing some release, he dismounted, let the reins hang loose, and walked a few feet away. Lifting his face to the sky he closed his eyes.

This raging desire for Juliet Ethridge was a complication he didn't need. He might have passed it off as a surface physical response, only he realized he liked her. She thought she'd been a coward to come here, to run from the man who'd fixated on her. All he'd had to do was recall how she'd bounced back, how she'd gone on with the rest of her evening, determined to not let the man interfere with her life any more than she could prevent. He lifted a hand and rubbed at the back of his neck.

It wasn't like him to get so tangled up with someone. He'd watched his father beat his mother before being a witness, in horror and fright, as his mother fought back. And kill her husband before she collapsed and died. Afterward, he'd lived with his aunt's constant caution about letting anyone get close enough to hurt. Too bad she hadn't taken her own advice. Then, he'd made the mistake of believing a woman wanted nothing beyond the loose connection they'd made. Only to watch in stunned sickness as she lost control of her helicopter while on a training mission.

Ending not only her life but that of their unborn child.

Although the Army deemed the accident as just that, the thought that his stunned response to the news had led to Chloe making a rash, fatal decision haunted him to this day.

"God, I'm sick of people dying." He moved back to the horse, mounted up and rode to Juliet's porch. He had no intention of lingering close to Juliet this morning. "Then, why the hell are you here instead of not going straight to the barn?" he muttered.

Taking the package out of the saddlebags, he knocked on the door, harder than needed but it felt damn good to feel the slight pain in his knuckles. Seconds later, he heard the click of the locks. And there she was. His irritation with the direction of his thoughts drained away. All he saw was her.

If she'd had trouble sleeping it didn't show. She surprised him by wearing a dress, something simple and loose. He could still imagine every curve under the material. Her feet were bare, her toes painted a soft pink. Her eyes were heavy-lidded, as if she wasn't quite awake although her lips, unpainted, curved slowly. Damn him, and her, he could picture her smiling up at him in just that way as he rolled over to make morning love to her.

"Good morning," she said in a voice he'd bet good money she used to convey sensual awareness in a character.

"I brought some coffee."

It did his mood no good to realize his hands trembled like a teenager about to pin a corsage on his prom date. He removed his hat and swept a hand through his hair. He was still getting used to it be longer than it had while he'd been in the Army.

"I thought maybe if I provided the coffee, you'd be kind enough to bring me a cup later this morning."

"I plan to work this morning."

"You take breaks, don't you?" He knew she did, had been informed it was something she did period-ically throughout the day in order to give her voice a rest or to read ahead and prepare for the next section of whatever she was working on.

He put his hat back on, tipped the edge with a fingertip. "If not, that's fine. I understand. After all," he added with a teasing smile. "I imagine you're used to ordering fancy coffee from some bistro rather than making straight black in a pot."

She took a small step backward in invitation. "I can make it now while I have breakfast if you want to come inside."

He didn't dare. His body was throbbing with the need to make a move, to press against her, sink inside of her. "I really should get busy."

She might be good with voices but she couldn't hide her feelings from her face. Disappointed dulled the brown of her eyes. "Okay. Will I find you in the barn?"

"There or in the corral."

"Can you wait for an hour, maybe an hour and a half?" she asked, confirming the detail he'd been given.

"Perfect."

"Walker," she called after he'd nodded and stepped off the porch. "I'd planned to buy some for you when I went to the store."

The simple thoughtfulness made his throat tighten. "Appreciate it."

Before he turned back to her and made a huge mistake, he walked to his horse and led it away. Work helped keep his mind straight. He'd forgotten how much he enjoyed horses and the satisfaction to be found with working with his hands. From his first tap of the keys in high school, he'd shown an aptitude for computer and electronic work. The Army had used that talent and honed the skill. Surveillance had been a natural next step.

This morning he used mucking out the stalls as cover while he hid cameras and listening bugs although he didn't imagine Juliet would find her way into the barn very often. He really needed some concentrated time in her house and studio.

The scent of approaching coffee alerted him as he completed the last installation. He was rubbing his hands over Captain's flank as Juliet appeared in the doorway. He didn't care for the way his heart hitched in his chest.

"Am I interrupting?" she asked.

"You are." He grinned and started toward her. "Thank God." His hand curled over hers on the mug. His gaze settled on hers. Heat that had nothing to do with coffee arched between them.

"You mocked my ability to make it straight black." Slowly she withdrew her hand from beneath his. "So I took you at your word."

"My aunt liked hers sweet and light so that's how I learned to drink it." He took a long sip. "The Army taught me to take it straight. Easier," he went on to explain when the question popped into her eyes. "Especially out in the field."

"And were you? Often in the field?"

"From time to time."

"You mentioned you enjoy electronics. Is that what you did?"

"Yes. I was an electronic warfare technician. Basically I analyzed, planned and implemented electronic warfare operations."

"So you weren't, what's it called, on the front lines?"

"No, I wasn't. I was safe in a tent while everyone else was out on patrols or missions."

She knelt down to stroke the cat when it rubbed against her leg. "I'm sorry."

"For what?"

"I'm not sure. Occupational hazard you could say. I know voices and I heard unhappiness in yours so I'm sorry for whatever put it there."

"I guess that kind of talent comes in handy in your line of work. How'd you get started?"

"I'm an only child of parents who both have demanding careers. Plus there's the fact that they were a little older than most couples when they finally had me. I spent a lot of time at the theatre and I just seemed to naturally pick up accents and ways of speaking."

"You didn't consider acting?"

Standing, she smiled, more pride than humor in the curve of her lips, in the glow in her gaze. "My mother is a Broadway legend. Would you want to compete with that?" She shook her head before he could answer. "I know if I wanted an acting career she'd have helped me in any way. But I was always more fascinated by technique rather than the actual act of acting."

"And you wanted to make your own way."

"Yes." She reached out, squeezed his arm in appreciation of his understanding.

He drained his coffee, set the mug carefully on a stall door. "You have a way of making me forget, Juliet. I should be thinking about work," he said, deliberately leaving his wording vague. "But all I can think about is wanting you, being with you. Taking you to bed." He heard her breath catch, saw it in the quick rise of her chest.

"I'm not the one who walked away last night."

He tunneled fingers through his hair, tugging on the ends a little. "This isn't what I planned."

"Finally, something we can agree on."

"Think," he commanded. "Think hard. Be sure."

He wanted to step closer, only his legs quivered as badly as a mare in heat. "Because if I touch you, I'm damn sure not walking away again."

She lifted her chin, defiance in her gaze. "No one said you had to."

"You deserve more than a quick tumble in the hay."

"I think that's for me to decide." She smiled, slowly, seductively. "And who said it would be quick?"

"Keep looking at me like that and we'll find out."

She tilted her head a little, studied him. "No man has ever wanted me the way you say you do."

"Then I can't say much for the men you've known."

"I can honestly say I've never met a man like you."

"I can't imagine you've run across many former soldiers now hired ranchers in New York City."

"It's more than what you've done or do with your life. It's you. All you."

She lifted her hands, pressed them to her chest. Right where he figured her heart pounded. It bothered him. Oh, not the wanting her. He couldn't stop that any more than he could stop breathing. But seeing her do that, the romanticism of the gesture, reminded him how very wrong he was for her. She was the kind of woman who wanted, deserved, a man who'd always be there for her. He wasn't that man.

Still, he had no intention of reminding her of that when he finally ended up in her bed, when he stayed with her throughout as many nights as they had. He could do the job that had brought them together without thinking long term.

He could keep her safe even if he eventually broke her heart.

CALM AND FOCUSED, Juliet worked the rest of the afternoon. Walker's attempts, both last night and today, to avoid the physical attraction between them touched a soft spot in her heart. He made no promises and she expected none. None that she would voice.

Still, her heart yearned. That at least was familiar.

Sometimes it seemed as if she'd been born yearning. Not that her parents didn't love her. Of course they did. Just as she loved them. But, from an early age, even before she knew of such things, she wanted the closeness she watched them share.

Just because a woman wanted intimacy didn't mean she couldn't have, from time to time, heat and speed.

She would have need, desire, passion, with Walker. There would, she guessed, be little patience between them. And that thought delighted her. She'd been honest when she told him no man had ever looked at her the way he did, that no man had said the things to her that he had. She was counting on him doing things to her no man had ever done.

No, she didn't know what it was about Walker that had awakened this reckless anticipation in her. But, God, her lips curved, she gloried in the knowledge that he had done so.

It occurred to her that what she was doing, planning, could be termed avoidance. Focusing on thoughts of being with Walker took her mind off worrying about Jon Hock knowing where she now lived. Too much of the last year had been spent with an eye over her shoulder. Or staying inside all together. She'd sheltered herself, as much for the protection of her parents as for herself. She came to Montana to regain her independence, to feel in control. What better way to cement that control than to enjoy a man who wanted to be with her?

Juliet pressed a pause button, read over the next few paragraphs in her current project, and then, after a long swallow of water and envisioning the scene in her mind, resumed her narration. She worked for another hour, spent time listening to the production, re-doing a section of the last chapter, and then decided she deserved a cup of tea. Setting her own hours, working at her pace although often on deadline, were perks of her job.

Going into the kitchen, she switched on the tea kettle and reached for her cell phone. Seeing the alert for a voice message confirmed her habit of not keeping the phone in the studio to avoid the risk of it interrupting her work. She didn't recognize the number but this was a relatively new phone so she assumed it was a robocall. Curiosity had her clicking to listen as she wedged the phone between her ear and shoulder so she could reach for a mug and tea bag. The voice that came through froze her actions and chilled her skin.

"Juliet, did you get my package? I had them send all of your favorites. I know what you like, what you need." There was a pause and she could hear his breathing accelerate. *"Soon, my love. Soon we will be together. Forever."*

Although a part of her wanted to do just that, she knew better than to delete the message. Instead she lowered the phone to the countertop with all the care she would use if handling a bomb.

Taking a few steps backward, she spun around and all but ran to the back door. Her hands trembled but she jerked the door open. All hell broke loose.

The alarm Walker had encouraged her to set now shrieked. The tea kettle began to whistle. Juliet, hating herself for the weakness, covered her ears, slid down onto her knees and rocked. Then all she knew, all she felt were strong arms folding around her. With her state of mind the tight hold around her should have frightened her. Instead she instinctively recognized him.

"You're okay." Walker nudged a strand of hair aside and whispered in her ear, "I've got you."

"It's never going to end. He's never going to leave me alone."

"He won't get to you." Walker kissed her temple. "I've got to turn off the alarm"

Her hands tightened on him. "Don't leave."

"Juliet." This time he kissed her softly on the lips. "I promise I'll be right back. Nothing is going to happen. You're safe."

When he silenced the alarm and switched off the heat under the tea kettle, her nerves ratcheted higher at the realization that her phone rang.

"It's the alarm company," Walker said, returning to her side. He answered. "Yes, this is Ms. Ethridge's home. No, there's nothing wrong. Ms. Ethridge opened the door without disengaging the alarm. Yes, of course, her password is *overture*." He nodded, ended the call. Juliet frowned at him, aware that something was off, but the reason wouldn't crys-talize in her thoughts. He framed her face in his hands.

"Tell me what happened."

"A message. On my phone."

He kept his gaze locked on her as he listened. She saw his eyes darken, narrow. His lips thinned to a hard line. His voice, after he punched in some numbers and spoke into the phone, giving someone instructions to try and track down the message he would be forwarding, was authoritative and direct. But, as he stroked a hand down her arm while talk-ing, he did so tenderly.

"Here's what you need to remember. The alarm did the job. It went off when you opened the door. I came." He reached for her hand, lifted it to his lips. "I will always come for you."

"Will you stay here tonight?" Not even embar-rassment prevented her from tightening her hand on his in a grip far stronger than her voice. "Not that way."

"I know," he said gently. "Of course, I'll stay if that'll make you feel safer. I will need to go over to my cabin, grab a few things. Would you like to come along?"

The panic that had risen in her throat with the thought of being alone, drained away. She hated feeling this helpless, this needy. Determined to re-claim her strength, she released her hold on him and inched away.

"That depends." She even managed a small smile. "Does it mean I get my first horseback riding lesson?"

CHAPTER 4

JULIET'S ANTICIPATION dimmed a little when she stepped outside. She knew it made no sense, but the horses hadn't seemed so large when they'd been in a barn stall. She'd thought Walker was tall, but standing next to the horses he looked undersized. Unless you took in the breadth of his shoulders and those long legs that led to a fine looking ass. She bit down on her bottom lip.

"Don't worry," he said, turning in time to catch her staring. "They're gentle."

"I guess I'll have to trust your word on that."

His eyes darkened as she approached. "I won't lie to you."

"Maybe," she said. "But can you guarantee I won't fall off and land on my butt?"

His eyes brightened, his lips curved in response

to her teasing. "No, but I'll be more than happy to rub your butt if you do. Of course, even if you stay on the horse, there's a good chance your butt will be sore by time we get back."

"And will you rub it then also?"

"Juliet." He lifted a leg as if to step forward, only to stumble when the horse, Scotty she recalled, bumped his shoulder. "Okay." He turned back, ran a hand over the horse. "Someone's anxious to get going."

"Not sure that makes me rest any easier."

"You'll do fine."

Walker reached for her hand, squeezed once before lifting it to offer the back of her hand to Scotty's nose.

"I'm hoping like hell you're not offering him a bite," she said, only to be charmed when the horse touched her hand with his nose. "Oh, aren't you a gentleman."

They spent a few minutes letting the horse get used to her. Then, with a deep breath, and Walker's hands on the back of her thighs guiding her, she mounted and settled in the saddle. She let out a sigh of relief when the horse remained still. Then, she watched in admiration for his grace and the flex of muscles as Walker swung up into his saddle.

She knew he set the slow pace for her benefit. He

also offered helpful hints such as hold the reins lightly, keep her knees loose and let her body move in tandem with the horse's cadence. Then there was the scenery. The land stretched out farther than she could see with streams undulating across the ground. Mountains, still snow-capped despite it being May, in the distance.

"It's like something from a movie set," she said, gently tugging on the reins and bringing the horse to a stop. She looked at Walker as he came up beside her. "I wish I'd thought to bring my phone along and take some pictures. My mother would love to see this."

"You're close to your mother."

"Very." Alerted by his tone, she asked cautiously. "What about your family?"

"I came here to live with my aunt when I was eight." He shifted in his saddle, nudged the brim of his hat up his forehead. "She'd already gotten out of one bad marriage and the man she was with at the time wasn't very good to her. As long as I didn't get into trouble, she mostly let me go my own way and do what I wanted. We got along okay, especially when the jerk wasn't around. Then, right before I graduated high school, she finally told him she'd had enough and he had to leave." If she had more riding experience Juliet would have reached over to take his hand. "A few days later she sat me down and said he'd somehow managed to get his hands on all her money. Some of that money had been left for me to go to college. Left with not much else to do, I joined the Army."

He rubbed the heel of a hand on his chest. "The guy, he, well, he got drunk one night and decided he didn't like that she'd tossed him out. He beat her. She didn't survive." He let out a long breath.

"I'm so sorry, Walker," she said, knowing the words were inadequate to ease the hurt of a young boy.

"The Army wasn't so bad." He looked at her, smiled a little. "Your butt going to hold up until we get back?"

Her chin lifted. "It will."

Barely. By time they returned to her ranch she was more than ready to end the experience.

"Need any help?" Walker asked as they stopped at the corral.

"I've got it."

Juliet bit down on her bottom lip to hold back the groan as she managed, and God alone knew how, to swing a leg over the saddle and touch ground. Her legs vibrated but she didn't embarrass herself by collapsing. She'd save that for when she arrived in her bedroom. Provided she could make it up the stairs.

"You sure you're okay?"

Juliet glanced over her shoulder to where Walker stood, releasing the straps on his saddle. Trying to subdue a grin.

"I am now. Tomorrow might be another whole issue."

"You should go upstairs and take a hot bath."

"With a cold glass of wine." She sighed, then paused. "Should I help you with the horses?"

"I've got them." He turned to her. "If you'll wait out here until I've got them unsaddled and inside the barn, I can walk inside with you. I'll have to come back outside and brush them, but they can wait a little bit."

"I'll be fine." She straightened her shoulders, using the peace she'd found on the ride to bolster her determination to not give today's phone call any more thought. "You stay out here and take care of them. After all, they have a couple of ladies to impress."

"They will," he said with a grin. "By the way, for your first time on a horse, you rode well."

Juliet smiled and made her way to the house. There, she spotted her cell phone still on the counter.

Defiant, she picked it up, saw she'd missed a call from her mother. Drawing in several deep breaths, in much the say way she would if reading a particularly tense scene in a book, she searched for calm.

"Hello, Momma," she said when her mother answered after one ring.

"You had me worried."

"Worried? Why?"

"I called hours ago."

Juliet relaxed and went to the refrigerator to pull out a bottle of white wine. "I left my cell phone behind. I really wish I'd had it with me. I would have sent you the most beautiful photos."

"Where were you?"

"On my first horseback ride."

The two women talked and laughed. Their ease had her thinking of how Walker sounded while talking about being raised by a stern aunt. Juliet mentioned nothing about either the basket delivery or the phone message. If she had, she knew well and good her mother would either come out here or send someone to keep an eye on her.

She was listening to her mother ramble on about rehearsals when the back door opened and Walker stepped inside.

Despite the fact that she'd just swallowed some wine, her mouth went dry. On some primal level that throbbed inside of her, she suddenly and desperately wanted to be alone with him. Fire licked along her nerves while liquid heat pooled between her legs. And, as close as she was to her mother, she didn't want to feel all this while talking to her.

"Momma," she interrupted. "I need to go. I'll call you tomorrow."

She cut the call, set down the phone and the wine glass.

He carried a backpack thrown over one shoulder, his jeans were dusty, and the top two buttons of his shirt had come undone, revealing a tanned chest with a hint of brown hair. She desperately wanted to undo the other buttons, run her fingers through that chest hair, tease his brown nipples into a hard nub with her fingertip. Take them into her mouth and suck. Trail her tongue down the center of his chest, trace the indentations of his flat stomach until she could finally dip below the waist of his jeans.

Until she could uncover him enough to take his dick deep in her mouth and drive him crazy.

Until he could plunge that same dick deep inside of her, over and over and over while she screamed with pleasure.

Because she kept her eyes locked on him the whole time, she saw him sling his hat aside and drop his backpack. Widen his stance in invitation as she walked his way. His arms folded around her, crawled up her back so his big hands could hold her head. He lowered his mouth as she rose on her toes, her hands gliding up his chest so her arms could lock around his neck. Their mouths met in a kiss that was almost savage in need and intensity.

Small explosions burst inside of her, drenching her panties in anticipation of everything she wanted to do with him. She moaned and felt no embarrassment at the needy sound. His tongue dueled with hers, loved hers, the way she wanted their bodies to mirror. His hands, oh God, his hands finally released her head and swept around to cup her breasts. Her knees went weak, both at the thrill of him cupping her and with the expectation of how those same hands would feel on her bare skin.

She felt his rigid erection pushing at her center. Her hands moved, dropping so she could cup him, squeeze through denim. His groan vibrated in her mouth. Encouraged, she began lowering his zipper.

"No." He jerked his mouth from hers, covering her hand to stop her. "I'm not taking you here in the kitchen." Before she could protest, before she could tell him she didn't care where they were as long as he satisfied this raging need, he smiled. "At least not the first time."

Then, he swept an arm under her knees, lifted her and carried her upstairs.

He kissed her throughout the trip, although his mouth gentled, his lips teased. Without hesitation, without direction from her, he strode into her bedroom.

"I've wanted you from the first time I saw you."

"Have me now," she said, her mouth running kisses over his face, down his throat. "God, hurry, please. I'm about to explode from wanting you." She ripped his shirt open, raced her mouth over his chest. "I'm not like this. I'm never like this," she panted, as he lowered her to the bed.

"Don't feel you have to stop."

"No damn way." She grabbed hold of the sides of his ripped shirt and tugged him down on top of her. Her legs spread wide to hold him so they were pressed center to center.

"Christ, I can feel how wet you are through these clothes."

"Take them off. Take them off."

"I didn't want it to be this fast," he said, even as he followed her demand and lowered her zipper.

"Next time we'll go slow." She lifted her hips as she damn near had an orgasm with the thought of him touching her. "God, touch me."

His hand slipped between the part of her jeans so

he could thrust a finger inside of her and his thumb grazed her clit.

She screamed his name as her hips rocked against him and the magic of his hand. Over and over he stroked her in a fast rhythm that matched the way her body erupted. One orgasm rolled into another until he finally paused long enough to strip off her jeans. Then it was his mouth, hot and hungry and relentless, as he feasted on her. Her head thrashed as he licked, sucked and teased her very core.

"Stay with me," he commanded as he rose above her.

"To hell with that."

Using strength in complete defiance of the way he'd depleted her, she wrestled enough distance between them that she could free him from his jeans. She loved the way his head flung back with her first long stroke, at the way she used a finger to tantalize by spreading his moisture around the tip. Compelled, she leaned forward and replaced her finger with her tongue before sucking his dick deep in her mouth. He wove his fingers into her hair, thrusting into her mouth with need that somehow escaped being harsh before swearing softly as he eased her away from him.

"Clothes, damn it," he said and levered off the bed to strip bare. Following his lead, she shed her clothes. When she looked up, he stood ready, condom already rolled onto his impressive length. Walker's gaze bore into her and she thought she saw a shadow of hesitancy.

Saying nothing, she held out her arms.

Her body opened, accepted and warmed with the way his dick filled her. There was no room for doubt, no miniscule inch to allow regret room to invade. His hips moved in a rhythmic roll that rubbed against her clit in a way that edged her toward another mind-blowing orgasm.

She bucked her hips in answer and provocation to his thrusts. Her legs wrapped around him, keeping him close. Her hands stroked down his back before they cupped his ass, marveling at the strength of muscle as he moved. Her mouth searched his, sighed when he kissed her with the same ferocious intensity as he fucked her.

They rocked together, at turns with speed and force only to settle into a gentle motion. It didn't matter how he moved within her, she responded. Twice more she climaxed before he finally lost control and thrust one final time in release.

Juliet lay still as her breathing levelled. Her mind vibrated with shock at her behavior. She had never been so inhibited, so demanding. So responsive.

So delighted and wonderfully exhausted.

With care, Walker pressed a kiss to her temple, to her forehead, her nose, and finally to her lips. "I'll be right back," he whispered, drawing fully out of her and going into the bathroom. She heard water running but didn't give it much thought beyond that of her own need to clean up. Her mind jerked awake when she felt his arms slid under her. With her head on his shoulder, she looked at him.

"I won't say I'm sorry," he said as he walked toward the bathroom. "But I do regret being rough with you. Especially so soon after your first horse-back ride."

She realized he'd not only filled the tub, but he'd lighted the candles she'd placed along the sideboard. Her heart went soft with tenderness at his gesture.

"You have nothing to apologize for. After all I'm the one who started everything." She cupped a hand to his cheek, pressed her lips to his. Smiled as she looked deep into his eyes. "And I believe you promised me a slow round the next time."

"I don't know if that's possible." He kissed her, long enough to have need stirring. "Now that I've had a taste of you, I'm greedy." Even as she felt him harden against her hip he grimaced. "Only I didn't plan for this. I'm not sure I have even one more condom with me."

"Then aren't you lucky I'm a city girl, raised by a

momma who taught me to be careful and prepared. Which means I'm never without my own supply of protection." She quirked an eyebrow. "Now let's take advantage of this bath water while it's warm."

He lowered her into the tub and she couldn't stop the moan of pleasure at the warmth that covered her. She caught his hand when he straightened. "Aren't you going to join me?"

"I'll be right back." He leaned down to give her a quick kiss. "I believe you said something about wanting a glass of wine to go with the bath."

"You don't forget anything do you?"

"Not where you're concerned."

As he left, Juliet admired his body and the ease with which he walked around nude. The instant he was out of sight, she closed her eyes and sank deeper into the water. If he kept saying things like that, treating her the way he had, not to mention giving her the most awesome sex of her life, she was going to fall hard for him.

Downstairs, Walker leaned on the kitchen counter and swore. He'd had no business putting his hands on Juliet. Or his mouth. And definitely not his dick. But, God, he reared back his head and closed his eyes, she'd been so responsive and open to whatever he wanted to do to her. She'd surprised, and pleased, him by making that first move, by being so aggressive and demanding. No way in hell would he be able to keep his hands or mouth off her now that he'd had a taste. How was he supposed to give her mother a report on Juliet's wellbeing without revealing he'd slept with her?

He shoved off the countertop, got down another glass, poured wine and headed for where the most delectable woman he knew waited for him.

Not only was she under his protection, and in real danger, but he didn't do involvements. He'd learned that lesson. The real problem was he liked her, admired the way she'd handled the stress of her stalker learning where she'd moved. He enjoyed her company out of bed as much as he'd enjoyed her body in bed.

He stopped in the doorway. She lounged in the big-ass soaking tub, her eyes closed and a small smile curving her lips. The water lapped over her breasts but he could see the dusky nipples beneath the water line. And lower to the hair covering her sweet pussy and the long legs that had wrapped around his hips as he pounded into her.

How the hell was he supposed to resist a sexy woman self-aware enough to have her own stash of condoms?

Damned if he would. His dick hardened in anticipation and he admitted he'd never have succeeded staying away from her.

"If I didn't know better."

Her eyes opened slowly, immediately dropped to take in his erect dick. She didn't move, simply continued to lie in wait for him to join her. "If you didn't know better?" she prompted after he'd settled in and touched his wine glass to hers.

"I'd swear you bought this tub knowing I'd want to be here with you."

"Can't say it crossed my mind." She sipped her wine. "Have you shared many baths with women before?"

His stomach clutched. "A time or two."

With a dreamy smile curving her lips, she moved her leg so she could stroke her foot up and over his thigh. "I remember once when I was a little more than five and waking up in the middle of the night. I went to my parent's bedroom but they weren't in their bed. That's when I heard laughter coming from the bathroom. They were in a jetted tub, so I'm sure the noise prevented them from hearing me."

"Christ, Juliet. You saw them?"

She laughed. "The tub was deeper than this one so I didn't really see anything but them sitting close together. It reminded me of the scene from my favorite movie at the time, The Little Mermaid, when Ariel and Sebastian are in the row boat. Especially when my parents leaned toward one another and kissed. I was so used to seeing them kissing all the time that I didn't think anything of it. I just turned around and went back to my bed."

She looked over his shoulder, as if replaying the incident in her mind. In her gaze he saw the kind of love she spoke of, the kind of love she'd grown up with.

The mother's love that had hired him to protect her daughter without her knowledge.

"Have you ever heard of the actress Vanessa Armstrong?" he asked.

Juliet's brows knit together as she sipped her wine. "Sounds vaguely familiar."

"She didn't make the kind of movies you were watching at the time. Her first, On The Run, was about a mother trying to find her two year old that had been snatched from the playground while she'd been assisting an elderly woman, who she later learned had been part of a baby kidnapping ring."

"Yes, I remember overhearing a couple of people discussing it once at one of my mother's parties." Her cautious tone, along with the way she studied him, didn't escape Walker's notice.

"She got rave reviews and everyone predicted she would become a star. Then she died. She was murdered by her husband." He met Juliet's gaze, saw the sympathy bloom in her eyes. "She was my mother."

"I'm sorry, Walker. It must have been awful for you. Is that when you came to live with your aunt?"

"Is that all you want to know? Or do you want to know how I felt watching my parents fight, as I'd already done countless times before, only this time my father slapped and pushed my mother hard enough that she hit her head on the edge of the fireplace hearth." He set down his glass, rubbed his hands over his face. "Or maybe you want to know about how my father yelled his apologies at me while he tossed the room to make it look like a robbery gone bad." He dropped his hands and stared at her. "Or how, before we could get out of there, I watched my mother stagger to her feet, blood dripping from her open head wound, and hit my father with a fireplace poker, killing him before she collapsed at my feet and died."

"Do you think hearing this story changes the way I look at you?"

"I come from violence. I came here to more violence." He swallowed. "I might have worked in a secure location, doing tech work, but I still lived with violence while in the Army."

Juliet placed her glass next to his and leaned

forward. "Walker, if anyone understands how a relationship can be used to hurt, it would be me. I'm here with you now because someone has twisted so-called love into something dark and dangerous. I trust you or I would never have been this intimate with you." She stood. Water drained down her body, dipping into and over the curves he'd had the pleasure to caress and trace with his tongue. She reached for his hands, drew him up so their bodies were close. "I don't want to waste any of our time together."

After they stepped out of the tub, he reached for a towel. With a smile she took it from him, dropped it on the floor. Like a barn cat lapping at milk, she ran her tongue over his chest.

"I'll get you dry."

Already rock hard, he stood still while she searched through a cabinet for her stash of condoms. Hand-in-hand, they went to her bed. This time there was no rush between them. Walker tried to shake off the feeling that her soft touches and slow riding of his cock were meant to soothe and calm. Even as they did. Afterward, he lay spooned against her back until he was sure she slept.

Then he rose as quietly as possible and went downstairs to betray the trust she claimed and invade her privacy by installing cameras and listening devices.

In spite of her acceptance of his past, he wouldn't, couldn't, consider making a commitment to her. After all, while he'd told her about his parents, he hadn't confessed about the woman he'd been with while overseas. He hadn't told her about the pregnancy and the resulting loss of the baby.

However, for the first time since meeting Juliet, he felt guilty for doing what had to be done to insure she remained safe from the man who wanted to hurt her.

CHAPTER 5

When the morning sun warmed her face, Juliet stirred. She grimaced a little at the discomfort she felt, only for her lips to then curve at the memory of how she'd become sore. She didn't have to reach around to know Walker wasn't in bed with her.

Just as at some point last night she'd awoken and knew he was gone. Before she could go in search of him he'd returned, his hand cupping and squeezing her breast. She'd turned to him, questions about his absence forgotten in the strong desire he so effortlessly awakened in her.

While it wasn't like her to have fallen into bed with someone after so short a time, she wasn't going to question her behavior. Nor was she going to make the mistake of believing last night was the start to a fairy-tale romance. What she and Walker had done last night was enjoy one another. Period.

If only her heart didn't stumble a little over that belief.

After showering and dressing she went downstairs. While she enjoyed a fortifying mug of tea, she watched Walker work with the horses. He moved with the same fluid power as he'd done last night while thrusting inside her, at turns gentle or forceful. She actually shivered when he paused and ran a hand up and down the leg of one of the horses. Desire tightened her belly, but she turned away and went into her studio. She had a deadline and while the sexy man tempted her to go outside and drag him upstairs or into the barn, she wouldn't let him distract her from completing the narration.

Hours later, she finally felt satisfied with the production. She'd enjoyed the twists and turns of the book and had to admit the storybook happy ending suited her frame of mind perfectly. Next up on her work schedule was narration for a nature film. Since that involved a different mindset from the project she'd just completed, she took a break.

Stepping outside she paused and once again marveled at the changes in her life. Maybe she'd come to Montana to escape a threat, but at the moment she had no regret for having made the move. The sky overhead showed blue with dots of white clouds rather than the spears of skyscrapers. And a hawk, she realized as she gazed up. The spring air brushing against her skin was cool and clean instead of clogged with scents of gas, sidewalk vendors and the crush of humanity rushing on every street.

Yes, she missed her friends and family. She would have no matter where she moved. At least here she had a serenity she hadn't realized she needed. Here she felt she could find the kind of life she'd always hoped to enjoy.

Walker stepped out of the dark interior of the barn, coming to a stop when he noticed her on the back porch. This was something, someone, else she needed. Not simply a physical need, although, God that was beyond anything she'd ever experienced. She wanted him, wanted to know his secrets, wanted to share his dreams.

She wanted a full life with him.

MORE DISTANCE than she could guess separated them, but she'd swear some kind of electric connection held them in place. Her breathing quickened, her pulse scampered. Her panties dampened.

They moved at the same time.

"I told myself I would stay away from you," he said, grabbing handfuls of her hair to hold her in place. His legs spread, creating the perfect space for her to nestle close to him.

"I worked all morning, ignoring you were out here." Her teeth grazed his chin, felt her muscles quiver at the rough texture he'd not shaved off. "No more."

He boosted her up so she could lock her legs around his waist. His mouth cruised over her face, finally covering her mouth in a smoking hot kiss. Her hips rocked to mimic the seductive impact of his tongue invading her mouth. Never before, with any man, had she felt this shameless and hungry. Only Walker had found the key inside of her to unlock sensual needs and desires that would have lay uncovered without him. Never again, with any man, would she feel this shattering passion.

"Where?" she demanded once she'd managed to wretch her mouth away from his. Only, before he could answer, she kissed him. "God, I'm going to come right here." Her hands rose to tunnel fingers through his hair. "Do something. Please," she begged as she leaned back so she could guide his face. His tantalizing mouth sucked through material, pleasuring her already hard nipple.

She bucked as the orgasm exploded inside of her. She had one brief clarity of thought to be thankful for his strength as she rocked hard and long. She was still vibrating when he moved.

"Juliet," he said, his mouth again claiming hers. "Damn, slow down. I've got to get us inside. Condom."

"Barn. Closer," she insisted.

"Condom," he repeated, growling at the way she continued to roll her hips against his arousal.

"I've got this. I'll take care of you."

He jerked once, but she claimed his mouth, preventing him from saying anything. She knew he wasn't ready for words, knew he wouldn't make a promise he couldn't keep. But she wanted, needed, to show him that what they'd found together could grow and become yet more. Until he was ready to hear the words, she'd use whatever means worked best.

Blinded for an instant between the bright outdoors and the subdued light in the barn, she held on to him. His muscles bunched and moved in a way that had her desperate for the freedom to explore and stroke all that power. She could breathe in the odor of arousal on him. A flick of her tongue tasted sweat and hard work. It all combined to have urgency pooling in her center.

He'd no sooner entered the tack room, where there was a small cot covered with a blanket, when she began tugging his shirt from his waistband. She groaned at the first feel of his warm, strong back under her hands. They curled around to trace and slide over his taunt abs, up to rub his flat nipples.

"God, I love your body," she whispered, sliding down to the rigid length of him straining his jeans. Her hands fumbled, then grew steady as she undid his belt and tugged down the zipper. Seeing the way his leg muscles trembled calmed something inside of her even as it spurred a renewed passion.

Before he could guess her intent, she freed and took him into her mouth in one swift, sure move.

Her lips coasted over him, her tongue laved and stroked and teased his tip. She licked the moisture that was his unique flavor. His hands cradled her head, urging her until they moved to cup her face as he tried to ease her away.

"Juliet," he groaned when she continued to suck and drive him toward release.

"Come for me," she murmured around his thickness. Curving her hands around his strong thighs she held him steady and pleasured him until he couldn't hold back.

"God, you surprise me," he managed between breaths as he stretched her out on the cot and slipped his hands under her dress and pushed the material toward her waist. "Hmm," he said, his mouth trailing open mouth kisses along the inside of her thighs as his hands urged her hips up and then drew down her wet panties. "I'm not finding a condom stashed here." His hot breath blew over her and she arched, desperate to have his mouth on her. Instead, he drew a fingertip down and into the drenched seam of her sex. He thrust several times, bringing her to the edge only to withdraw.

He smiled at her groan when he eased back, just enough to curl her legs over his broad shoulders. "Come for me," he repeated her demand, returning his mouth to her. She screamed his name when she did.

"Why did you leave the Army?"

Walker jerked, Juliet's question rousing him from his sated relaxation with her tucked close to his side. If anyone had told him that he'd have a sexy woman, especially a woman from her kind of class background as his lover, he would have sworn that person was a liar.

"I'm sorry," she said, confirming she'd felt his

automatic tensing at the inquiry. "Never mind, I shouldn't have asked. It's none of my business."

His hand moved to cup her face, to tilt it up to his. Far more gently than his heart pounded in his chest, he kissed her.

Maybe it was the sexual coma she'd put him in, or simply Juliet herself, but he wanted to tell her, give her the one truth he'd never told anyone. There was so much he couldn't, wouldn't say to her. This at least he could reveal. Besides it would do both of them some good to be reminded of how lousy he was with relationships.

"I told you about how messed up my parents were with each other. Then I came here and my aunt wasn't exactly the warm and fuzzy type." She remained silent, looking at him, her brown eyes filled with a depth of trust no one had ever given him before. "Since all I'd ever seen were relationships that ended up with someone getting hurt I promised myself that I'd never get involved."

"Do you think that's why I asked?" she whispered. "Because I expect a commitment from you now that we're lovers?"

"No." He pressed his forehead to hers. This wasn't the first time he felt as if she'd somehow shifted the mood, had somehow altered the direction of the conversation. She somehow managed to make him believe she cared. "At odd times I think you expect too little from me."

"I only expect as much as you're willing to give." She ran a hand down his spine. "I'm very lucky, Walker, to have parents who adore one another, who love me. I'm not ashamed to admit I hope someday to find what they have. That doesn't mean I haven't seen my share of how people can hurt one another."

"You could never hurt anyone."

"Oh, but I could." The hand stroking down his spine, paused, pressed a little. "Who was she, Walker?"

"Chloe Thomas." He blew out a breath. "She was a helicopter pilot, primarily she flew rescues. Part of what I did was provide intel for her flights. We were enjoying one another, hooking up whenever our schedules allowed. I told her from the beginning that we would only be together as long as we were deployed at the same duty station. She'd grown up in foster care so she said she didn't expect anything from anyone. She was used to being on her own."

"Only, she wanted more."

He paused, not sure how to go on. This would be the hard part of the story, the part where he revealed it hadn't been his finest moment. The part where he exposed himself to the guilt and shame that had haunted him since that day. As if understanding his misery, she shifted the hand at his back up to cup his cheek, her thumb stroking in silent support.

"Everything changed when she told me she was pregnant." Juliet's thumb stopped, then resumed stroking again in an easy rhythm. Her eyes looked deep into his, revealing the loss she had yet to hear about but somehow guessed was coming. "She'd stopped taking her birth control pills without telling me. We argued. She knew how I'd felt about relationships, knew I was only with her for the time we were stationed at the same base."

He rolled off the cot, turned his back to her. "I didn't love her, asked her how she expected me to trust her after she'd done something like this. Still. . ." He blew out a breath, lifted a hand to rub at the center of his chest. "There was some part of me, a part I never knew existed that got a kick out of being a father. I don't know why since I didn't have any experience and definitely didn't have a good example in my past."

He turned back to face Juliet, suddenly wishing he'd put on his pants so he could shove his hands into the pockets. "I promised I'd support them both financially, but I needed some time to think, to decide what else I would give her. I'll never forget the look on her face before she left."

Juliet rose, went to him, tears brimming in her eyes. Unable to stop, he reached for her hand.

"Two days later, as I sat in the operations tent, relaying instructions and coordinates while she flew a mission, I watched the radar as she crashed." Juliet's eyes closed and a tear slid down her cheek. "The Army investigated of course, determined that it was the result of a mechanical issue. I'll always believe I was to blame."

Juliet's eyes snapped opened, surprising him with the fury he saw there. "She's the one who betrayed your trust. You never lied to her, Walker." He winced, knowing how much he'd kept hidden from Juliet.

"I'm sorry you lost that chance to be a father." She leaned over so she could press a soft kiss to his lips. "I know better than some that it's easy to look backward and see where or when we might have made a different decision. Only there's no guarantee that decision wouldn't have disappointments or losses also." She smiled a little. "All we can do is appreciate what we have while we have it."

"And when we don't?"

"We cherish the good memories and move on," she answered.

While a part of him relaxed with her easy acceptance that they had no future together another part of Walker hated the way she seemed willing to move on without him.

FOR THE NEXT WEEK, they each went about their individual work. When their schedules allowed, they ate lunch together, often talking about books or him asking questions about her narrating, mentioning what he'd done around the ranch. Neither brought up the subject of Jon Hock.

Juliet often thought of Walker's confession, his surprised idea of wanting to be a father, even as she tried hard to not imagine his child growing inside of her. While he spent nights in her bed, a future of being together, of having a family together, was a level of commitment he wasn't ready to consider.

She didn't want to settle for less than a full, loving commitment, had always promised herself she never would.

"You look deep in thought."

She jerked upright in her chair. Then, when she looked over, her heart jerked hard in her chest. Walker leaned against the doorframe, his arms crossed over his chest. His jaw showed he hadn't shaved that morning and he had a small smile curving his lips to go with the glint in his eye. She recognized that look. Her body warmed to that look.

"I was thinking of my lover, Andre." With her heart hammering, she gestured to the phone beside her, speaking with a French accent she'd used once in a book narration. "He called, lamenting that it has been far too long since I traveled to France to be with him."

"That so?"

"Oui. He adores me."

"I went to France once. Met this woman." Deliberately, oh she knew he did it deliberately, he said nothing more, leaving her imagination to fill in the blanks. It galled her to recognize the sudden flare of jealousy and yet she could do nothing to tamp it down.

"Is that so?"

"Yep." His eyes darkened a little. "I can't whisk you off to Paris, but I can offer you another horseback riding lesson. If you have time."

She smiled. "It so happens I'm free at the moment."

They had a lovely ride, one during which they talked and laughed. Walker spoke of his childhood more freely than he had before, telling her stories of his first horse, the dog he'd wanted but his aunt refused to have in her house. When they stopped at a small pond, he surprised her with a blanket and a light lunch. After eating she stunned him by stripping naked and entering the pond. She'd sucked in a surprised breath at the chilly water, then moaned when he finally joined her.

The next day, at her work station, she again moaned. Only this time with no pleasure in the sound. Nor in the pit of her stomach.

"No, no, no." Juliet stared at the sound board with the same distress she imagined a doctor encountered while watching a patient die on the operating table. She lifted her hands, only to pause before she touched any of the controls.

She'd just spent the last two hours doing some of the finest work she'd ever spoken. Now she couldn't find it anywhere on any of the formats or recordings. What the hell had she done?

Nothing she maintained, staring at the equipment, hoping against hope some miracle would occur and she'd see what she needed to do to retrieve the narration. Lights beamed back at her, slides remained fixed in place, and the display screen showed ready for recording.

Only she believed she'd been recording throughout the work. She'd been pushing through this job, hoping to clear her calendar in case the deal for the animated movie came through. That had to be why, she rubbed her eyes, she thought she'd seen a quick image of her bedroom before the screen went blank.

"Damn it."

More than frustrated over losing some of the finest work she'd done, she would now have to cancel her evening with Walker and spend it doing narration she thought she'd nailed solid.

Rolling her chair away from the controls, she huffed out a breath and, hoping a break and free air would clear her mind, walked outside to sit on the back stairs. Her heart stopped dead in her chest when she spotted Walker, shirtless in the warm sun, as he chopped and stacked firewood for winter. She'd been looking forward to going to dinner at Avery and Daniel Sawyer's. Not only would it get her out of her house to meet her new neighbors, but it would give her a little break from the intensity of her feelings for the man that had caught her eye.

"Oh, hell," she muttered. "Just admit it, he caught more than your eye. You're half in love with him."

It was more than the physical attraction, although, damn that was strong. He claimed he was essentially a loner and yet from the stories he'd told and the phone conversations she overheard, he had many friends and always had time to talk when someone reached out. He'd done more than take care of her livestock and finalized the details for the upcoming horse breeding. He worked her ranch as if it was his, leading her to wonder why he didn't have a place of his own. Was it because of his belief, his insistence, that he wouldn't be tied to anyone?

He didn't mind helping with the cooking, although, her lips curved a little, he usually found a way to avoid the clean-up. It seemed a fair trade to her. Often during the past week, she'd come out of the studio to find he'd poured her a glass of wine and they'd talk about their day while relaxing on the rocking chairs on the front porch.

In bed . . . as much as her feelings went beyond the physical, she admitted she'd never before felt so cherished and needed as the way Walker made her feel.

So, why did she have this gut level trepidation that something was off?

She thought part of it was not having heard anything from Jon Hock in the past week. While she wanted to believe he'd given up his obsession with her, she knew better than to relax or believe herself safe. Still, she knew she could survive any physical threat the author might impose. She wasn't as confident of her resiliency should Walker end their affair.

Maybe it would be best after all if she spent some time alone tonight.

"Hey." Juliet looked up, so deep in her thoughts that she hadn't been aware of Walker walking her way. "You done working for the day?"

"Apparently not," she grumbled.

"What's wrong?" He sat beside her, close enough that she could smell the odor of sunshine, horse and sweat, not close enough for her to put distance between them.

"I can't find the recording I finished this morning."

"What do you mean you can't find it?"

"I can't find it," she all but shouted, then drew in a deep breath. "Sorry. I'm frustrated because I don't know what I did wrong."

"You're always meticulous about saving your work as you go along. It's got to be there somewhere." He stood. "I'll take a look."

"Walker." She hurried after him. "Look, I appreciate the offer and I don't want to hurt your feelings." She stopped when he looked back at her.

"I told you, I know electronics," he said, and pushed into her studio. "Nice equipment." After a quick scan of the room, he sat and immediately began pushing buttons, turning dials, working the keyboard of the computer. Juliet edged closer to watch over his shoulder. She watched his fingers practically fly over the keys, saw the rapid screen change on her computer, cursing once under his breath.

"Here it is," he said, his hands stilling, hovering over the keyboard.

"What?" The idea that she'd once again seen a flash shot of her bedroom vanished under her astonishment and delight. He pushed a few keystrokes and her voice filled the studio – in perfect sync with the video in her computer screen. "You found it." It hadn't been a question or even a comment. More like a prayer of thanks. He gave her some technical jargon, explaining why she hadn't been able to find it. All she cared was she didn't have to repeat the entire narration. "I owe you."

"Yeah?" He smiled at her, rising and pulling her into his arms.

"Walker." She wrinkled her nose. "You need a shower."

"Yes, I do." He began walking her backward, out of the studio. "We'll save time if we shower together before we head over to Avery and Sawyer's tonight." His lips trailed up and down her throat, his teeth nipped at her chin.

"Oh, I don't think so," she said on a choked laugh that morphed into a moan when his hands slipped beneath her top.

"Besides," he said, cupping and squeezing her breasts. "You owe me for finding your work."

She gave up trying to protest. She admitted she'd been wrong – she'd never done anything half way in her entire life. What made her think she'd do anything less than fall into full blown love with Walker?

JULIET LIKED AVERY SAWYER. The woman had an easy, relaxed manner in spite of keeping an eye on her adorable son Cole, running a ranch, and exchanging smoldering glances with her attentive husband. Which no doubt explained her pregnancy bump.

Right now, however, the men – adults and child – were talking horses in the barn while the women remained in the kitchen. And, oh, as Cole giggled when Walker had lifted him to ride on his broad shoulders, her heart had ached with longing to have, in spite of his instance that he was no good at relationships, a family with him. Avery refused Juliet's offer of help, asking only that she sit, enjoy a glass of wine and conversation.

"I'm in awe," Juliet said after her first sip of cold

white wine. "That you took care of all this while raising such a cute son on your own."

"It wasn't just me. I had Carl and Esther. And Randy." Her eyes darkened a little before she lowered a hand to her belly. "But it's easier since Daniel came into our lives."

Juliet grinned as she toasted her glass in the direction of Avery's belly. "So I can see."

Avery blushed. "How did you two meet?"

"Meet? Don't you know? I mean. I'm sorry, I guess I thought you knew."

Suspicion skated down her spine. "Knew what?"

"I was being threatened." Juliet immediately set down her glass and reached for Avery's hand.

"I'm so sorry. Were you hurt?"

"I received threatening text messages, was run off the road. Daniel and I were shot at." Juliet's hand tightened. "Randy." Avery's breath hitched. "Randy kidnapped Cole."

"Oh my God."

Avery smiled. "Daniel rescued him. We knew where he was because Daniel had a tracking chip placed into a dog tag he had made for Cole." Avery tilted her head and considered Juliet. "Walker's the one Daniel asked to make it."

"Walker?" Juliet blinked, sat back on her stool. "I

thought you and Walker knew one another from high school." Avery nodded her head in agreement. "Did he and Daniel know each other from the Army?"

"No, they met through Hank Patterson."

"Sadie's husband?" Juliet slid her glass away a little. Obviously the wine was going to her head. "I don't understand."

Avery looked down, concentrating on slicing carrots for salad. "I guess you could say Hank has a way of introducing guys that can help out one another from time to time. Hank knows Walker is talented with electronics." She set down the knife, brushed her fingertips along a towel, and then reached for Juliet's hand. "C'mon, I still have some pictures of Walker from high school."

Several hours later, after saying good-bye to the Sawyers, Juliet still chuckled over Walker's embarrassment at discovering she'd seen his high school photos.

"I can't believe she showed them to you," he complained.

"You looked good in your tux." Juliet lifted her head from where she'd been cuddling against his shoulder and studied his profile. Even in moonlight she could make out his features, the eyes that constantly scanned the surroundings, the strong jaw prickly with evening beard, the lips that could coax or demand a response from her.

"You look good now," she whispered. He glanced her way, his right brow lifted. "Did Avery sit beside you like this on your prom night?" He shrugged, avoided her gaze. She touched the tip of her tongue to her bottom lip. "Did you park somewhere so you could make out before you took her home?"

"Cut it out, Juliet."

"You did." Charmed by his embarrassment, she grinned, lifted a hand to run a finger down the buttons on his shirt. "I've never made out in a car before." Leaning over she used the tip of her tongue to flick at his earlobe. "Stop the truck, Walker."

"We're almost home."

"Stop the truck."

"Look." He groaned a little when her hand trailed down to stroke over his erection. "We're too old to act like a couple of randy teenagers in a truck. You have a perfectly good bed at home."

She used her teeth to nip at his ear, and a thrilling hot lick of lust sped down her center when she felt the truck increase speed. "I want you now."

"How am I going to explain to your mother that I wrecked this truck because her daughter had her hands all over me?"

Juliet laughed. "If you meet my mother, she'll probably say it's your own fault for hesitating."

He swore as he braked to an abrupt stop under the motion light near the back door of the house. Juliet didn't wait, she gripped his face in her hands and, suddenly greedy, devoured his mouth with hers.

"God, I love kissing you," she said.

"Shut up."

As she did so, as mouths tormented and enticed, as tongues tangled and promised, heat steamed up the windows. They each swore as he struggled to release his seat belt and get his hands on her. She giggled when, while trying to climb onto his lap, the horn beeped. Instead, he scooted them over the bench seat, pulling clear of the steering wheel, giving her room to straddle him. While she ground her pelvis into his erection his hands rose to cup her breasts. She arched her throat, giving him access to lick and nip, sending shivers of delight down her back. He was right, they'd have more room in her bed. But, God, she couldn't wait, didn't want to wait. Saw no reason whatsoever to wait. She had a sexy lover right here within reach.

She made quick work unbuttoning his shirt, stroking her hands over his sweaty chest. Before he could repay the favor, her cell phone exploded with the hit song from her mother's latest Broadway hit.

Walker jerked his mouth from hers, pressed his forehead to hers and breathed hard. Even as he kept his hands on her breasts.

"My mother." Juliet heaved in and out a breath. "Walker, I'm sorry." Welcomed lust transformed into concern. She swallowed hard, working to keep it from blooming into fear. "She should be at the theatre."

"Answer it."

That innate understanding, that willingness to set aside a heated moment, confirmed for her they had more than lust between them. Neither one seemed willing to say anything concrete, to ask for more, but they were connected by an invisible, unexplainable bond. She scrambled to move off his lap and reach for her phone. It stopped before she located it, then immediately began to ring again.

"Momma?" Juliet drew in a breath, scooped her hair away from her face. "What's wrong? Why aren't you at the theatre? Is it Daddy? Is he sick?"

"Juliet." Her mother's sharp tone stopped any more questions. "Jon Hock sent me a photo of you."

Juliet went stock still. "What kind of photo?"

"Are you at home?" There was a humming second of silence. "Outside, sitting in a truck?"

Puzzled, Juliet frowned and stared at Walker. The fact that he wordlessly left the truck unnerved her.

That he drew a pistol from his back waistband rattled her further. Through the windshield she watched him walk the perimeter, his head turning as he investigated every dark corner. "Yes. How do you know?"

"I'm sending you what I received."

The ding to indicate a text message buzzed in her ear. Juliet put the phone on speaker and with two clicks brought up her mother's message. A photo, grainy yes but still clear enough to give her mother a distinct image of her daughter in a passionate embrace with Walker came through. What had her blood freezing was the bold lettering, in blood red, written at the bottom of the photo.

Slut! Why would you do this to me?

"How." She swallowed, shuddered. "How can he do this?" She looked up from the screen, stared out the windshield, searching for any sign of someone watching. "How does he know what I'm doing? No matter what I do, where I go, he's never going to stop."

"Juliet." Her mother's calm tone stopped her from erupting into a full-blown panic attack. "Take a deep breath, darling. C'mon, do it." Her mother continued to soothe. "You can face this. You're stronger than he is." A hint of amusement crept into her words. "And your very attractive date looks like he can protect you. Oh hush, Ron. She's a grown woman. Plus, we raised her right." Margot chastising her husband did more to relax Juliet than a hundred words of instruction.

"Momma." Juliet bit down on her bottom lip as Walker climbed back into the truck. "Daddy," she said and, against all reason for why she was on the phone with her parents in the first place, grinned at the way Walker paled. "Walker's back in the truck with me."

CHAPTER 6

WALKER SWALLOWED DOWN THE OATH. Damn if he would give Juliet any reason at all to suspect he'd spoken with her parents before tonight.

"Walker," Ron Ethridge demanded through the speaker phone Juliet had activated. "How the hell can this monster have live video of the two of you?"

"Sir. My guess is he hacked into Juliet's security system. Or knows someone he could hire to do it for him."

"I thought you were an electronics expert. Shouldn't you have been able to prevent this?"

"Wait." Juliet laid a hand over Walker's. "Daddy, how do you know Walker has experience with electronics?"

"Because," Margot said into the half beat of silence. "Once you told us that he was working

there, living on your property, we had him investigated."

"Mother." She lifted a hand to rub over her face.

"Darling."

"Juliet," Walker cut off Margot's attempt at soothing. "It's okay. In their place, I would have done
the same."

"There," Margot said, obviously satisfied the
matter had been resolved. "Now, what are you going
to do next?"

"I'm going to find out how the bastard was able
to circumvent the system." He drew in a ragged
breath. "First I'll alert the local sheriff. If that doesn't
keep the jerk away, I'll call in every favor I know to
track him down and then beat the shit out of him."

"That sounds like a workable plan," Margot said.
"Keep a close eye on my girl."

"Not too close," Ron said in the second before
Margot cut the call.

Walker counted off the seconds before Juliet
whirled on him. Three, it took three seconds. Her
eyes glowed with equal parts fury and embarrassment. He could only imagine which part would
hold once she learned her parents had hired him to
keep that close eye on her. Of course, they hadn't
planned on him having his hands on her. Neither
had he.

He damn sure hadn't planned on having thoughts that included a future with Juliet beyond this job.

Didn't the fact that they sat here now, with her security being compromised, prove he had no business thinking along those lines? He had to re-focus his attention away from the delectable temptation of her and concentrate on keeping her safe.

"Do you want to tell me what's going on?"

"C'mon," he said, opening the door and exiting. He held out a hand for her to slide across the seat and follow. "Let's get inside."

She slid out but didn't reach for his hand, walking toward the house without a backward glance in his direction. Just as well. He needed the silence and time to figure out how to handle the situation. And Juliet.

Once again he thought this was a perfect example of why he had no business getting tangled up with a woman.

When he stepped into the kitchen, she stood leaning back against the counter, a glass of wine lifted to her lips. Lips that were swollen from the hot, tempting kisses they'd so recently exchanged. Lips that could skate over his skin and make him feel things he'd never known was possible to feel.

With no effort he could picture looking like this while at a society gathering in New York. Yes her hair was messy, by his own hands, and he could just make out the faint white knuckle grip of her hand on the wine glass. Still, she stood, wanting answers. The trick would be in giving her answers without telling her everything.

"How did Jon Hock know my mother's phone number?"

"With the same kind of ingenuity he used to learn your address and hack into your security system would be my guess."

"Speaking of that. When did you put up cameras? I assume there are more than one."

At his sides, his hands closed into tight fists. "I won't apologize. Not for the cameras. Not for doing whatever it takes to make sure you're safe."

"I don't recall asking you for an apology. I simply want a timeline."

"Right after that first delivery." Walker stepped forward. His earlier admiration for her strength and guts turned into anger at her calm front. Damn it, he knew she wasn't as controlled as she wanted him to believe. He'd seen and heard the panic in her voice as she spoke to her mother. But she'd regained her composure quickly, and had gone on to express her trust in him to her parents.

God, he wanted her. Right here, right now.

"Show me." She set down her glass, straightened her stance.

His entire body jerked, thinking she'd somehow read his mind.

"Show me how many and where they are," she said, dragging his mind back to the situation at hand. Every trace of fear had been replaced by determination. Courage. The woman had it in spades. God, yes, he wanted her.

While he'd do everything possible to make sure she remained safe, he was also more scared than at any other time of his life. She meant too much to him. Somehow he'd allowed her to get close enough to matter. For the first time since he lost his mother, he didn't want the casual or temporary. He wanted Juliet and the life they could make together.

Only, he knew without a doubt that when she learned her mother had hired him, when she learned he'd never told her the truth, she'd be furious. Somehow he'd have to find a way to make her understand. Because now that he'd found someone worth fighting for he had no intention of going away.

JULIET DID her best to ignore the sensation of being

watched. She tried convincing herself that because she knew about the cameras it was only natural she'd be aware of their presence. During the two days since Walker showed her the cameras, she'd struggled against looking up at them. Shoved aside thoughts of the invasion of her privacy. A camera even in her damn bedroom. Her cheeks flushed at the idea of what Jon Hock might have seen there before Walker installed new security measures to block any further hacking. She frowned. Now that she thought about it, she realized he'd never answered her questions about payment for the security measures.

He claimed he had no interest, and less success, when it came to relationships. And yet he'd done so much to make sure she felt safe and protected. Was it any wonder her heart beat hard and fast and full for him?

Needing a break, she shut down her work, blew out a breath. And looked over at the new screen. In grainy black and white, she watched Walker, stripped down to a T-shirt that revealed those marvelous muscles in his arms, rub a soothing hand down Captain's forehead. She didn't hear but saw his mouth quirk with laughter when Scotty came over to butt him in the shoulder, wanting his share of that same gentle touch.

He had such gentleness and compassion in him. Did he not see it, recognize it, because of seeing the way his parents had fought until the violence killed them? Then he'd come to live with an aunt who struggled to find her own emotional stability and thought only to provide basic living conditions. Someone who encouraged him to leave at the earliest possible time?

Why could she see what he had to offer? Because her parents had given her love, acceptance and faith throughout her life so naturally she saw it, cherished it, in others?

Why couldn't he see that she would do the same with him?

They could build a life together, become partners. Make a family.

On screen she saw Walker's head jerk up. Her throat closed when the front bumper of a delivery truck came into view. But she stood and went outside.

"That's mine," she declared, intercepting the package before Walker could claim it.

"Juliet."

"I want to see." With a grim smile she signed the delivery form and thanked the driver. She faced Walker. "I need to know."

"I'll come with you." He hesitated. "If you don't mind."

Balancing the package in one hand, she reached for his with her free one. They didn't speak as they entered the kitchen, nor when she used a small paring knife to slit open the package. Her hands trembled, making her stop and draw in a deep breath, before she pushed open the box flaps. Nestled inside a foam padded insert perfectly molding it, she stared down at the glass replica of two calla lilies blooming snow white and cool on a grass-green stem. She didn't reach for them, didn't stroke a finger along the fluid lines of the beautiful piece. She didn't need to reach for the card wedged at the base to read the message.

You will always be mine.

"He used this, I mean, the antagonist in the book I cancelled the narration on, used it. He sent a figurine exactly like this to torment the heroine. Days before he abducted her. Before he sexually abused her."

"He won't lay a hand on you."

"You can't promise that." Strangely she felt dead calm. "And I won't live my life constantly looking over my shoulder."

It nearly amused her to see the way his eyes narrowed. He might claim to want no relationship, he did in fact continue in small ways and few words to remind her he believed so. But standing here now, seeing that fierce, protective gleam in his gaze, she knew he cared for her. Maybe not to the extent that she loved him, but far more than the 'it's just a physical attraction' claim he insisted they shared.

"I trust you," she said. "And I know you'll do everything you can." She lifted her shoulders and let them fall. "We'll be careful but the reality is all we can do is wait for him to make his next move." She leaned over, lightly kissed Walker. "I'm going back to work for a bit. Be careful out there."

"Juliet." He gripped her arm, then closed his arms around her. His lips grazed her temple. "I'll do more than everything," he vowed. "I'll do whatever it takes."

She angled her head, pressed her mouth to his for a short, satisfying kiss. Then she stepped back and walked into her studio without a backward glance.

She came out several hours later to tempting scents of tomato sauce and garlic, a set table, complete with candles, and a sexy man, with his own tempting masculine, clean scent, pouring wine.

Seeing him in her kitchen preparing dinner, and the small touches he'd gone to the trouble to do, reminded her of her earlier thoughts about how generous and kind he could be. How considerate it was that, after her long day of narrating, or perhaps in self-defense of her barely tolerable cooking ability, he didn't mind working in the kitchen. Just as he tended the livestock and property. And then there was the warmth and gentleness he used while making love to her.

Maybe he had kept the truth about the cameras from her, but with a little time she could accept he'd done what he thought was best. What he believed was in her best interests.

Her breath caught as the feeling swelled up inside her, burst out before it could be blocked or tempered.

"Walker." He turned, smiled. And the words poured out. "I love you."

The smile vanished. She fought to ignore the ache. Only, as with the love, there was no way she could ignore it.

"I don't expect anything," she hurried on, then blew out a long breath. "Well, I think I could really use that glass of wine." She closed the distance between them. "From the look on your face, I think you'd do better with a shot of whiskey." She took the glass from him and, keeping her gaze locked on his, took a long swallow. "Don't worry." Another sip, even though the first was already burning in her stomach. "I understand neither one of us expected my feelings to grow to this point. But I also won't lie about my feelings. You've been honest with me from the beginning." She leaned in, much as she'd done earlier today.

"I've never expected anything more from you than you're willing to give. Because my feelings grew doesn't mean we can't continue as we've started." She touched her mouth to his, reassured by the warmth of his mouth accepting hers. "Now, what are you cooking that smells so delicious?"

"Juliet, if I could."

Her smile trembled when he stumbled to silence. The tears that wanted to slip free were ruthlessly tamped down. "Okay, one last confession. You can, Walker." She lifted a hand to cup his cheek, held his gaze steady with hers. "You're the only one who believes otherwise."

FOR THE REST of the evening Walker worked at keeping Juliet's declaration out of his mind. He figured stress and perhaps a sense of misplaced gratitude had her believing she loved him. Certainly she acted no different than usual during the rest of the night. Following the meal she'd done the routine clean-up while he went outside for a final walk around the animals.

His electronic searches told him Jon Hock hadn't been spotted since the day he'd sent the photo to Margot and Ron Ethridge. Not knowing where he was made him itchy. After some thought he decided to confess her mother had hired him to protect her. He hoped Juliet would understand and she would accept her mother meant well.

Before he could find the right words to start the conversation Juliet seduced him with a sweet fierceness that told him she held tight to her earlier declaration of love. Promising himself he would confront her in the morning, he took all she gave him, all she accepted from him, until they both slipped into a deep sleep.

Walker woke at his usual early hour. He considered waking Juliet. Rather than have the conversation he'd avoided the night before, he rationalized morning chores needed to be handled first. Once they were taken care of he would go to her and explain everything. With a last look at Juliet sleeping, he turned his back and left the bedroom.

In the barn, he blanked his mind to everything but chores. He didn't want to think about what he'd say, what explanations he'd give. He didn't want to sound rehearsed, didn't want to come off as cold and mechanical. God knew he didn't want to think about her reaction or responses.

"This is why I should never get involved with a woman," he muttered, returning to the barn after leading Captain and Scotty into the paddock.

"Juliet's mine."

Startled, swearing, he swung around. Jon Hock, short and dressed in black, his eyes wide and wild, approached from the shadows of a stall. Before Walker could reach for his gun, Hock plunged a knife into his shoulder. He then swung out with a shovel, catching Walker on the temple, followed by a shove into his stomach. Neither were strong enough to drop him, but when Walker attempted to reach out and disarm him, Hock drove the end of the shovel onto the wrist of his injured arm. Walker heard bone snap and went down on one knee, his vision blurring as Hock leaned over him. He gritted his teeth against a roar of pain when the author twisted the knife before he jerked it free and kicked him to the ground.

"You'll never touch her again," Hock declared.

A vicious kick to the ribs was the last thing Walker felt before he passed out.

~

Juliet hurried out the backdoor. "Walker?" she called out just inside the barn. As her eye made the transition from summer sun to barn dimness a soft fur brushed against her leg. Kneeling, she ran fingers over Molly's back. "Well, I haven't seen you in a couple of days. Are you thinking a short walk will encourage those babies to show up?" She continued petting the silky fur, cupped a hand around the bulging belly. "I'm sure you're uncomfortable," she murmured, low enough that Walker wouldn't hear. "But I envy you. Soon you'll have babies."

"I'll give you babies."

Startled, and with the cat darting away, Juliet jerked, her feet going out from under her. She plopped onto her butt, felt the phone she'd stuck into her back pocket not give way. Hoping it hadn't broken, and that she'd be able to access it, she looked up into the eyes of Jon Hock. Eyes that blazed with madness. Panic shifted into fear when she saw the knife he held.

And the blood on the blade.

Bile rose in her throat, and her heart thundered in her chest. Her breath wanted to race in and out of her lungs and for one revolting spin of her stomach she feared she might vomit. She fought the instinct to jump up and run. Or attack. Neither would help Walker. She prayed he could still be helped.

"Hello, Jon," she said, sickly pleased with how calm she sounded. Her legs held when she rose to stand. "You should have told me you were planning to visit."

He grinned and she had to lock her knees to keep from collapsing. "I didn't want to ruin the surprise."

"Surprise?"

He lifted the bloody knife as answer. "He won't get in our way anymore."

Her mind veered away from the image his words created. Instead she fought to remember tactics from some of the thriller books she'd narrated. She'd use whatever means, however fragile, she could if it meant helping Walker survive.

"He was never in the way." She hoped Hock believed the jerk of her shoulder to be nothing more than disregard. "He was little more than a diversion, a respite you could say, from the boredom of living out here in the wild."

"You came here."

"Yes, because I needed quiet to work."

"You refused to read my books. I haven't been able to write since," he whined like a two-year-old. Tears flooded the eyes that pleaded with her. She looked away, sick to her stomach at the thought of how much time was speeding by, time during which Walker could lie bleeding to death. That's when she spotted the rake Walker used for mucking out the stalls. The tines looked sharp and lethal.

She took a careful step toward Hock. "Why don't we go inside my house? We'll have a cup of tea while we talk about your book." She gestured with one hand that he should move toward the door. The other she stretched to see if she could reach the rake. Only she reached too far, stumbled and knocked the thing to the ground.

"What are you doing?" Hock demanded, moving toward her. His tears fell now. "Isn't it enough that you hurt me by ignoring me? Now you want to wound me. Why?" he asked, clamping a hand on her arm, twisting hard enough to make her cry out. "I love you. I would have given you everything."

Then, suddenly, she was shoved free. In horror she watched Walker waver on shaky legs, giving Hock time to slash the knife across an arm already red and wet with blood.

Before she could spring forward and grab either the rake or his arm, Hock slashed out at her. The blade point nicked her arm. He cursed as he turned back to Walker.

"This is all you fault. She would have loved me if not for you."

"No. She would never have loved you."

"Yes she would." Hock lunged. Walker jumped

back to avoid the tip of the knife, staggered and reached out to grip a stall door to steady his legs.

Against everything quivering inside of her, Juliet remained silent so as not to distract. But she knelt down and picked up the rake, ready to attack should there be enough room to do damage to Hock and not injure Walker any further.

The two men lunged at one another, wrestled for control. In spite of a hand slick with blood, Walker clamped it over Hock's wrist and gave it one hard twist. Hock cried out but didn't drop the knife. Walker inched closer, his face a study in concentration, fury and determination.

"She belongs with me," Hock gritted out.

"No, she doesn't."

"You'll never have her."

"I know."

With one last desperate cry, Hock shoved at Walker with his free hand. Only Walker somehow managed to keep his grip and pulled the man with him. They landed on the ground, Hock on top of Walker. With a grunt, Walker jerked the arm holding onto the knife upward.

Hock's mouth gaped open when he lifted his eyes to her. She would forever claim she saw the life literally drain out of him. When Walker rolled him off, she saw the blade plunged in the gaping wound of his stomach. Walker lay on the ground, struggling for breath, his shirt soaked with blood.

For what felt like an eternity but could only have been seconds, she stared and fought the panic, desperation and fear. Then, she lowered to her knees beside Walker. His chest rose and fell in shallow breaths. What she experienced now was so different, so much more than when she'd faced Hock. Before she'd been worried about getting away, getting help. Now she worried she'd lose the love of her life before she could contact anyone.

She was deathly afraid she would lose him before they had a chance at the life she wanted and he was too damn stubborn to admit he wanted as well.

"Don't you die. Damn you, don't you die." She jerked her phone from her back pocket, noted the cracked screen and punched buttons to call for help.

"Juliet." She blinked at the faint voice, so different from what she was used to hearing from him, and looked down to see his eyes were glazed, his face ashen. "I'm sorry."

He passed out and, after leaning over to kiss him, more to confirm he still breathed than anything, she stripped off her shirt and pressed it to the wound on his shoulder until help arrived.

CHAPTER 7

Juliet refused to leave Walker's side. When the sheriff and medics arrived, she continued to stay close by, using a blanket they'd given her to cover up. She climbed into the ambulance before they could tell her no, before the sheriff could detain her for questioning. With a sigh, one of the medics passed her a T-shirt while his partner worked to stop Walker's bleeding.

After a ride to the hospital that felt hours long she followed the gurney, stopping only when a steely eyed nurse held her back. Feeling helpless, Juliet closed her eyes and the nurse pulled her toward a curtained area. There she had her cuts and bruises looked at, had her vital signs logged on a chart.

She blinked when the curtain parted, expecting

the sheriff. Instead a tall, broad-shoulder man walked in.

"Hello, Juliet. I'm sorry we have to meet under these circumstances. I'm Hank Patterson, Sadie's husband. How are you holding up?"

She swallowed, the fear scraping down her dry throat. "How's Walker?"

"They've got him in surgery. He lost a lot of blood."

Her stomach revolted at the memory of all the blood on the barn floor, on her hands and shirt. On him. Biting down on her bottom lip, she willed the nausea to settle. "I'll donate. I can." Hank placed a gentle hand on her arm to keep her from jumping off the exam table.

"We've got plenty of people doing that. The doctor I spoke with said Walker should come through the surgery."

"And Jon Hock?"

"He's dead."

She felt nothing – no relief, no regret for having a man lose his life in front of her. "Walker had to kill him. It was self-defense."

"I know." He squeezed her arm a little.

"I don't understand why you're here." She lifted a trembling hand to rub at her right temple. "Why isn't the sheriff asking me about what happened?"

"Tell me first."

"Why?" She wanted to shake her head, wanted to try and clear away the fuzzy sensation clouding her thoughts. On the other had it seemed only fair that she deal with a headache and some mild confusion while Walker was in such pain. "Why should I tell you?"

"You can discuss that with your mother. She's on her way. And your father."

"My parents? They're coming here?"

"Yes." He hesitated. "I thought you'd want them here with you so I called them." When she continued to stare at him in silence, he reached back and parted the curtain. "Nurse, can you get Ms. Ethridge something for a headache, please? Now," he said when he'd turned back to her. "Talk to me."

She went over everything from when she rose that morning to stripping off her shirt and pressing it against Walker's wound. When the nurse popped in with some medication, she hesitated.

"You don't want Walker to see you in pain."

"But he'll be in pain." She sniffed back tears. "Because of me."

Hank smiled a little. "He'll be loaded up on meds. And you know he'll never blame you."

"Alright," she said and swallowed the medication. "Is there anything else you want to know?"

"I think you've covered it."

"Can you check on Walker and let me know what's happening?"

"Of course." He again took her hand, guided her to lie down. "You rest while I'm gone. I'll be right back," he said when she opened her mouth to protest.

Alone, she closed her eyes and let the tears fall.

She must have dozed off because her body jerked with recognition at the voices coming down the hall. She'd just struggled up to sitting when the curtain was thrown back in dramatic fashion.

"Momma."

"Oh my darling."

Margot Ethridge hurried into the small space, swept Juliet into her signature scented embrace. The familiarity and comfort of her mother's hug had Juliet weeping again. Her father sat beside her, wrapped one long arm around her shoulders.

"You cry, my darling, you go right ahead and cry."

"You came." Juliet hiccupped as she gathered her composure. "How did you get here so quick?"

"I chartered a plane."

Juliet stared at her father, stunned. "You what?"

"I wasn't about to wait at some airport for hours while my baby was alone." Margot shivered. "I'm so thankful you weren't hurt."

"Walker was." Tears again rose to spill over. With a smile, she accepted the linen handkerchief her father pressed into her hand. She'd never known him to be without one. "He lost so much blood. No one has given me any update on him."

Her father rose. "I'll see what I can find out."

"Now." Margot patted her daughter's shoulder before she turned to her handbag. "Let's get you prettied up before you see your hero. The man deserves a bonus."

"What?" Juliet stopped her with a hand to her arm. "What did you say?"

"Ah, just that he deserves a reward for what he did." She swept a powdered brush on her daughter's cheeks. "I owe him for my daughter's life."

Juliet rubbed at her throbbing temple. This wasn't the first time her mother, or Walker for that matter, said something that had her questioning what she couldn't quite put her finger on. Before she could pursue the thought her father reappeared.

"He's out of surgery and in recovery."

Thankful for her father and whatever strings he no doubt pulled, Juliet slid off the bed. "I want to see him."

Her father held out a hand. "I told them you would."

HE HAD MORE color on his cheeks than when he'd been bleeding on the barn floor, but he still looked pale. She'd expected the machines and yet they tore at her heart. Pulling over a chair, she sat, closed her hand over his. And waited for him to wake.

It was almost two hours before he stirred. Any attempt to get her to leave his side was met with stubborn refusal. Juliet shot to her feet, stroked a hand over his cheek. "It's okay. You're all right, Walker." She lowered her mouth, gently, to his. "I'm here."

"Safe." His lids fluttered open, closed. His chest rose with a sigh. "You're safe."

"I'm fine." She leaned close. "My parents are here." She kissed his cheek. "My mother thinks you deserve a reward."

"No." His eyes opened, stared at her with a dull regret she wanted to believe was caused by medication. Only a cold certainty told her differently. "Your mother already paid me."

WHILE JULIET FOLLOWED a nurse's directions to a private conference room, she recalled snippets of conversations. Her mother teasing her about meeting a handsome cowboy, how he'd known the passcode to her security system, her father mentioning his expertise with electronics. Her mother's assertion he deserved a bonus.

When she eased inside the conference room she stared for a long moment. Her parents sat knee-to-knee, holding hands, whispering. As close as possible for two people to be outside of an intimate setting.

Even as her temper simmered, her heart softened. This is the way she'd seen them her entire life – devoted, united. They argued, she knew they did. Two strong-willed people were bound to have differences. But they always found a way to connect. That type of bond was what she'd hoped to find in a partner. What she'd believed she had a chance of having with Walker. Only it had all been a ruse, a role portrayed in the name of protection.

Heartsick, she took a step forward, the movement alerting her parents.

"Darling." Her mother took a step, then sent her husband an annoyed glare when his hand stopped her. "Did Walker wake up? Were you able to speak with him?"

"He's the one who had something to say."

She'd intended to sound strong, accusatory.

Instead she heard notes of confusion and betrayal in her voice.

"You hired him."

"Yes, and I'm not at all sorry that I did." This time she managed that step forward, her face set in fierce lines that did nothing to diminish the resolve. Or the love. "There is nothing I wouldn't do to keep you safe."

"I love him." Her laughter carried more bitterness than humor. She hated feeling this way toward her mother, knew in her heart that her mother had done what she thought best. It still grated on her, the secrecy of both her mother and Walker. "Small wonder he didn't handle that well when I told him. I'm sure that wasn't a line item in the package plan."

"Juliet Allison." The command in her father's voice had her snapping her face up to his. "I understand you're upset, but you will not speak to your mother that way."

"But it's okay for her to interfere in my life? To treat me like I'm a toddler?"

"To treat you," he answered. "Like the child we both love with every beat of our hearts."

Juliet stared at them, united, as they so often were. Although it still grated a little, she accepted why they'd hired Walker, accepted, as always, their love and devotion. In the end, what could she do but forgive them? Embrace them. Still, the knowledge that Walker had been spending time with her because he'd been hired to do so stung her pride.

Reassuring her parents that she was fine, she finally convinced them to go to her place and get some rest. In spite of the circumstances, Juliet smiled as they left the conference room, as nurses and staff recognized her mother. She knew she'd upset her mother, knew her mother worried about her emotional well-being along with Walker's recovery. And yet, Margot Ethridge warmly signed autographs and smiled for photos. At the end of the hall, her parents looked back, sent her a small wave before stepping onto the elevator.

Juliet walked to Walker's room to sit beside his bed and wait for him to wake.

HE KNEW she was there before he opened his eyes. It wasn't that he could smell her lotion over the hospital odors, enjoy the glory of her body pressed to his rather than the stiff bed linens, or feel the warmth of her hand holding his. He just knew.

He'd become so accustomed to her. Could no longer imagine his life without her. He'd been a coward, too afraid to risk disappointment, too confined by the past to consider a future. And had nearly lost his chance with the woman he loved.

"Juliet," he whispered past a dry throat and parched lips. The silence surprised him. He'd been so sure she was here.

He felt sweat pop out on his skin as he struggled to open his eyes. Damn it, he hated being this weak. After what felt like ten minutes of work, he turned his head and there she was.

The beep of the monitor transmitted his increased heart rate. He wasn't sure what he'd been expecting – maybe tears balancing on her long lashes, exhaustion and worry creasing her forehead, or hands knotted in her lap. Instead he got a firm line of lips and a hard glint in her eyes.

"What's wrong?"

"What's wrong?" She practically flew out of the chair, all but quivering as she stood stock still. Pessimistic, he realized why there was no worry or tears in her eyes. Instead they blazed with temper. And hurt. "I trusted you."

"Give me a chance to explain," he said, fighting to sit up, collapsing when his body refused to follow orders.

"Why? So you can lie to me some more?"

"I never lied to you." He hated this weakness, wanted to pound his hands against the bed. He wanted to reach out to her, draw her into his arms and hold her. "I didn't tell you the entire truth but I didn't lie."

"You can call it anything you want. The end result it the same." She drew in a breath. The hurt shining in the eyes that had so often looked at him with love sliced at him more viciously than Hock's knife had. "I believed you when you said you were tending the livestock."

"I did," he managed, disgusted by his labored breathing. He refused to acknowledge the nasty streak of panic that had sweat pooling at his back. The beeping of the monitors picked up again. He wasn't surprised when the nurse came into the room. Juliet crossed the room to stare out the window.

"Good to see you awake, Mr. Grant. Are you in any pain?"

"No," he answered, despite the heavy boulder lodged in his chest. God, he hated feeling this helpless, not being able to go to Juliet, hold her while he explained. He thought if he could just hold her, he'd find a way to explain everything.

The nurse fussed a little, straightening his sheet and adjusting the tilt of the bed, and checked his vitals. "I'll let the doctor know you're awake." At the door, she glanced from him to Juliet. "Try and remain calm."

"You spied on me," Juliet said, barely above a whisper once they were alone.

"No, I set up security surveillance as a way to protect you."

"Because my mother paid you."

"Initially, yes."

"Initially? Does that mean payment stopped once you slept with me?"

"Hell, Juliet. You have to know that I didn't sleep with you because I was being paid to. That's an insult to me, you and your mother."

"Then why did you sleep with me? Oh, wait, that's right, it was just sex." She turned around to face him. "You made it quite clear that I shouldn't expect any kind of relationship with you. No wonder you were horrified when I said I'd fallen in love with you." She crossed the room, heading for the door, not once looking his way. "At least you don't have to worry about that anymore." She jerked the door open, hesitated but still didn't look back at him. "I'll see that my mother takes care of your hospital expenses." Now she looked at him and the pained emptiness in her eyes stabbed him in the gut.

"There'll be no need for you to return to my home. I no longer want you in my life."

As he watched her leave the room, Walker

resisted the urge to call after her. Just his damn luck that the only time in his life when he wanted to run after a woman and ask her, beg her, to be a part of his future and he was too weak to make the first move.

He didn't have a clue how in hell to convince her to give him a second chance, but he had no intention of giving up.

IF ASKED, Juliet would swear she was a terrible liar. But for the past week, her life had revolved around one lie after another. Every time one of her parents asked how she was holding up, she told them she was doing fine. When Avery came by to check on her, she lied about how grateful she was to Walker for saving her life.

She lied to herself every single day and night about not wanting him in her life.

"Good morning."

Juliet glanced up from the cold cup of tea she'd been staring into. "Good morning," she said, still lying because nothing had been good since learning her mother had hired Walker.

Her mother breezed into the studio as if strolling

onto stage. "I have the most marvelous news." She sat, smiled at her daughter.

"We're going to be working together."

"In what way?" Juliet asked, too far gone into her misery to see the worry that lurked behind her mother's carefully made face.

"You know the animated movie you were waiting to hear about? Well, my agent just called. I've been asked to do the voice for one of the minor characters."

"But, I haven't been notified if I've been hired or not."

Margot leaned in and squeezed her daughter's hand. "Act surprised when your agent calls."

"Oh, Momma."

The first beam of happiness she'd felt in days seeped into her heart. She was being told, on the sly, that she was about to learn of the biggest boost to her career. Plus, she'd have the joy of working with her mother.

"We should celebrate." Margot rose. "Surely you have some champagne. We'll have mimosas."

Juliet stood. She wasn't getting anymore work done today than she had any other day. Why not take the time and spend it with her parents before they returned home? For not the first time in the past week, she considered leaving Montana and returning to New York. Or maybe she'd move to California.

It wouldn't matter. Wherever she went, a part of her heart would stay here. With Walker.

"Where's Daddy?"

"Oh, he's outside." Margot paused, then touched her tongue to her top lip. "He had some questions for Walker."

Juliet stopped, pressed a hand to her suddenly jittery stomach. She prayed the hand would also keep her from running outside and jumping into his arms. "Walker?"

"Yes." Margot continued walking into the kitchen. She chuckled as she opened a cabinet, drew out a pair of crystal champagne glasses. "I think your father's living out some sort of childhood fantasy of being a cowboy."

"I told Walker not to come back here."

"I admit I worried about whether or not he should be doing manual labor so soon. But your father told me he's managing just fine." While Juliet digested this bit of news, her mother went to the back door. "Ron," she called out. "You and Walker come inside. We're celebrating."

"Mom," Juliet hissed. When she turned to leave, she felt a hand clamp down on her arm.

"You weren't a coward when you faced down that

man," her mother said. "Don't be one now."

Rallied by her mother's words, Juliet nodded and turned to the cabinet to pull down two more crystal champagne glasses. She didn't need to hear boots on the floor or smell the odor of outdoors to know he'd come inside. She felt her heart quiver, then spread wide, as if holding her arms open for an embrace. Juliet closed her eyes, only to have flashes of Walker fighting with Jon Hock to burrow into her mind, followed by images of Walker bleeding on the barn floor. Walker in the hospital bed, his eyes dark as she skewered him for what she saw as his betrayal.

Walker smiling at her with encouragement during her first horseback ride. Walker sitting in the bathtub he'd drawn for them, explaining about his parents, believing she'd think less of him. Walker rising over her as he thrust inside, giving her more, so much more, than physical pleasure.

"What're we celebrating?" her father asked.

It took more strength than she thought she possessed to stand by, acting, while her mother explained the impromptu celebration. She accepted her father's congratulations along with his hug and kiss on the cheek, tried to argue she'd yet to hear formal word that she'd be offered the voice over job.

Her heart racing, she faced Walker. His eyes were

soft as they searched hers. The open collar of his shirt gave her a peek at the bandage he wore.

"I'm happy for you," he said, touching his glass to hers in a toast.

Before she could say anything, the phone in her studio rang. Proving she was indeed a coward, she hurried away. Even hearing she'd just scored the biggest job of her career didn't spark any light inside of her. Avoiding her parents, she locked the door of her studio. And wept.

The next morning she entered the kitchen to discover a box of tea sitting beside her favorite mug. Walker was the only person she'd told about the new flavor she wanted to try.

Two days later, she stared at a silver chain holding a horseshoe charm.

The next day she found the DVD of a favorite movie she'd overlooked when packing for the move to Montana.

A new book waited for her the next morning. She smirked at the romance cover even as her heart softened.

While she stood there, considering what to do, she felt her mother close hands over her shoulders and walk her to the window overlooking the back yard. There she saw Walker kneeling in a newly turned patch of dirt, planting an assortment of flowers. The gesture was such a contrast to the cold glass lilies Jon Hock had delivered to her.

"He's courting you, Juliet," Margot said. "He's taking the time to give you something that will remind you of him. That's not the behavior of a man who only paid attention to you because he'd been hired to do so. Trust your heart that fell in love with him. And trust his." Her mother's hands gently squeezed. "Don't make either of you suffer any longer."

Juliet turned, rose on her toes to kiss her mother's cheek. Then, she walked outside.

The only sign he gave of knowing she'd come outside was the briefest of pauses in the planting. Gentle, she thought, his hands were gentle as they pried the bedding plant loose from the container, as he placed it in the hole and then used that gentle hand to spread soil over it. How often had she watched those same hands tenderly handle one of the horses? Or the barn cat? Her?

It struck her as exactly the sort of thing he would do. For someone who claimed he wanted no ties, he was taking the time to plant roots. With little effort she could imagine him cuddling their baby with that same tenderness.

"You shouldn't be working this hard. It's too soon." She bit down on her lip. "After your injury."

"The doctor cleared me." He released another plant from a container, tapped it into the ground. "And this is soothing."

"Have you been in much pain?"

His hands stilled and he lifted his head to look at her. "More than I believed possible." Tears blurred her eyes as he stood. "I won't apologize for doing whatever it took to keep you safe. I will apologize for not telling you sooner about your mother hiring me. I hate that you'd think for a single second that I pretended interest as nothing more than a way to protect you. The truth is I couldn't imagine not being with you. Not just your body, but your mind and soul and your heart." He dusted his hands together, then, swearing, lifted them to press the heels against his eyes. "Christ, Juliet, he had his hands on you. For the rest of my life I'll live with that. With what might have happened if I hadn't gotten there in time."

"No. Don't." She moved to him, pulled his hands away. And saw something in his gaze that she recognized only too well. Something that gave her hope.

"I love you," he said, his mouth seeking hers.

It wasn't the hurried, intense kiss she might have expected. But, oh, there was need, floods of it. The need to give, the need to forgive, the need to share, the need to love.

"Give me a second chance," he said, kissing her again, wrapping his arms around her. "Please, God, don't send me away."

"I tried to send you away. I tried to forget you. I failed miserably." With her hands framing his face she kissed him. "I've missed you so much."

"I've never loved anyone before you." He lifted his head, stared deep into her eyes. "I'm afraid I'll do something to screw this up."

She grinned. "I'll tell you if you do."

"Don't I know it."

His smile faded as he sucked in a breath. She saw a flicker of unease and then his gaze cleared. Her stomach jumped, but with excitement.

"You're everything I never knew I wanted. And now I don't want a life without you. I love you, Juliet. Marry me. Please."

It was so simple, so lovely. It was everything she'd ever dreamed of being said to her. It filled her with hope and faith in the future. In them.

"You're everything I knew I wanted. I love you, Walker. Of course I'll marry you."

He pressed his lips to her temple, held her close before he reared back, lifted his hands to cup her face and looked deep into her eyes. "I hope you don't want to wait too long before we start our life together."

She smiled. "How does tomorrow sound?"

He kissed her, long and thoroughly. "Perfect."

AT THE WINDOW, watching her baby girl being kissed by the man she loved, Margot smiled when the love of her life wrapped his arms around her. She settled back against Ron, covered his hands with hers, thankful for the thrill that had barely diminished throughout the years.

"How long do you think we'll have to wait before they give us grandchildren to spoil?"

DANIEL'S CHOICE

Pam Mantovani

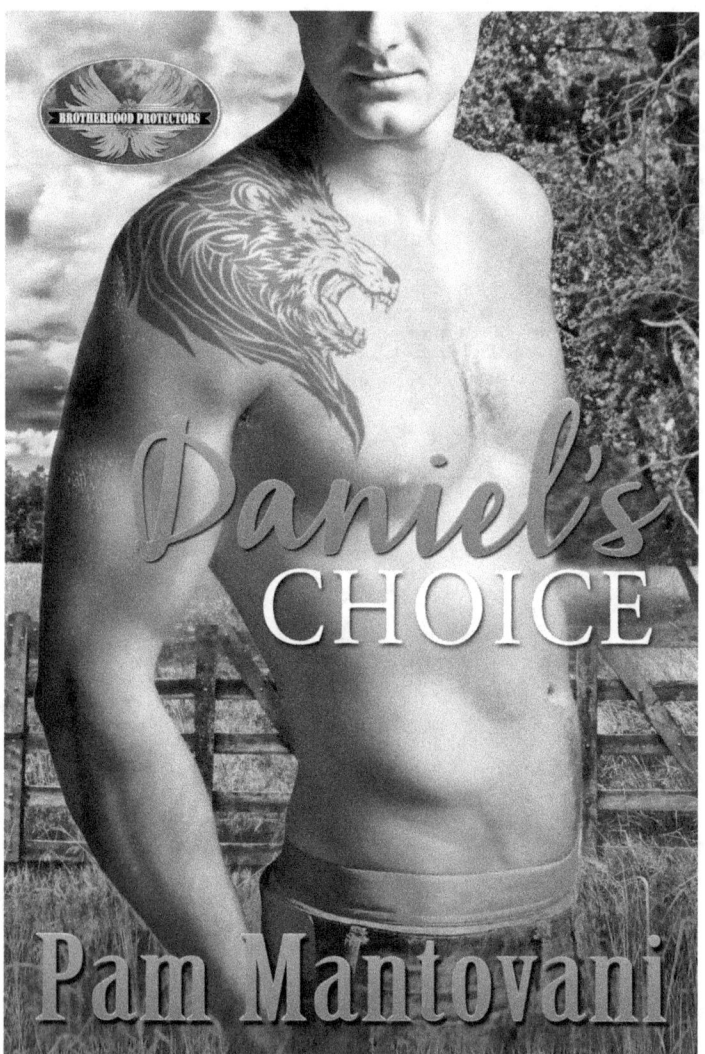

BROTHERHOOD PROTECTORS

Daniel's CHOICE

Pam Mantovani

Brotherhood Protectors

"You're wearing a gun."

"And I will until I put an end to the threats against you." He stepped closer, crowding her even as she refused to back away so much as an inch. "I've been hired to protect you. And your son." She knew he'd added that last bit to goad her. Still, she couldn't argue when Cole's safety mattered more than her own. "What I've not been hired to do is this. But, I'll be damned if I wait until I'm done before I do."

With his hand curling around her neck, he pulled her against his hard chest. She looked up, seeing in his gaze his intent to kiss her. He hesitated, long enough for her to voice denial or push him away.

Banding her arms around his waist, she shivered when she grazed the gun at his back. Moving her hands lower, she cupped his ass as she rose on her toes.

And had her world rocked to her core.

She wasn't a virgin, and even before she'd had her first lover she'd kissed several boys. Nothing in her experience prepared her for the feel of Daniel's mouth on hers.

He all but devoured her. His lips were firm, demanding, as he covered hers. As he had hers opening, inviting, accepting, making demands of her own.

This was no sweet, soft seduction. This was insistent passion refusing to be calmed. This was a kiss promising all kinds of naughty ways to make her body explode. She moaned a little, tightening her hold on the hard muscle of his ass, craving the climax his kiss incited within her. She nearly boosted herself up to wrap her legs around him so she could have, even through layers of material, the glory of his thick arousal satisfying her. Or, her dizzy mind considered, she could drag him to the floor, not caring one whit where they were, how long they'd known one another, or who might come upon them.

Only, that someone would be her son.

Like a cold splash of water in the face, the realization hit her, stopped her. She jerked her mouth free of his. Her hands were slower to get the release message. Daniel's fingers relaxed but didn't relinquish his hold on her neck.

"I probably broke one of the Brotherhood Protector rules," he said, the claim soft under his labored breathing. His eyes remained locked on hers, searching for how she felt about his behavior. "But damn if I can care."

"Since I was a more than willing participant, I could hardly ask that you be removed."

He smiled, and a part of her wanted to throw caution to the wind and reach for him at the way his face changed from dark and dangerous to open and inviting. "Willing participant, hell. You practically jumped me."

"I wanted to."

Her bold statement had him taking a step forward. The loud clomp of small boots on the stairs stopped him.

"He's your first priority," Avery said, reaching out a hand and clamping it around his wrist. Her palm covered the cording and brass in the bracelet he wore. "I don't care what you and Hank discussed. If it comes down to a choice between Cole and me, you choose my son." Her fingers flexed a little. The needs Daniel had ignited within her were quieted for now by her concern for her son's safety.

"Promise me that you'll choose my son."

Barnes and Noble: http://bit.ly/2k83544

Kobo: http://bit.ly/2kwXnas

SHARED SECRETS

Amazon: http://amzn.to/29reioM

Barnes and Noble: http://bit.ly/2kYcA57

Kobo: http://bit.ly/2ltgyzr

CRYSTAL CLEAR:

Amazon: http://amzn.to/2kNsYW9

Barnes and Noble: http://bit.ly/2lvIpA4

Kobo: http://bit.ly/2kTtO3M

ORIGINAL BROTHERHOOD PROTECTORS
SERIES

BY ELLE JAMES

Brotherhood Protectors Series

ABOUT ELLE JAMES

ELLE JAMES also writing as MYLA JACKSON is a *New York Times* and *USA Today* Bestselling author of books including cowboys, intrigues and paranormal adventures that keep her readers on the edges of their seats. With over eighty works in a variety of sub-genres and lengths she has published with Harlequin, Samhain, Ellora's Cave, Kensington, Cleis Press, and Avon. When she's not at her computer, she's traveling, snow skiing, boating, or riding her ATV, dreaming up new stories. Learn more about Elle James at www.ellejames.com

Website | Facebook | Twitter | GoodReads | Newsletter | BookBub | Amazon

Follow Elle!
www.ellejames.com
ellejames@ellejames.com

facebook.com/ellejamesauthor
twitter.com/ElleJamesAuthor